Passion's Liberation

Book 1

Khushi T. Saha

Edited by Jessica Gang

Book production by MysticqueRose Publishing Services LLC

Acknowledgements

Writing isn't easy, but it can be cathartic. What began as a self-awareness project turned into something much bigger than I could've ever imagined. I want to thank my editor and publisher for taking the time to walk me through the process and breaking down the intricacies of working on a piece of literary fiction.

I would also like to thank my family for giving me the experiences that led me to want to put pen to paper. Most importantly, I thank my husband. Without his patience and love, I would never be who I am today. Without his encouragement, I would never believe in myself to do this. Thanks babe. You're one in a million.

Contents

Acknowledgements iii

PRESENT DAY, NEW YORK CITY...7

Chapter 1 8

FIVE MONTHS AGO, LONDON 15

Chapter 2 16

Chapter 3 23

Chapter 4 30

Chapter 5 42

PRESENT DAY, NEW YORK CITY...51

Chapter 6 52

FIVE MONTHS AGO, LONDON 59

Chapter 7 60

Chapter 8 68

Chapter 9 75

Chapter 10 86

Chapter 11 92

PRESENT DAY, NEW YORK CITY..105

Chapter 12 106

Chapter 13 123

Chapter 14 130

Chapter 15.. 140

Chapter 16.. 149

Chapter 17.. 167

Chapter 18.. 187

Chapter 19.. 193

Chapter 20.. 204

Chapter 21 221

ধন্যবাদ 232

Present Day,
New York City

⌒

Chapter 1

Early Fall in NYC, and Marcus was back. He pushed through the hotel revolving doors and took stock of The Plaza's cavernous lobby. Shiny marble floors, vaulted ceilings with gold cornicing and oversized crystal chandeliers met his gaze. Stylish groups of hotel guests stood or sat, chit-chatting here and there in immaculately spaced sitting areas; either waiting for rooms to be ready or heading off on expensive city excursions. How many times had he stayed in this luxurious hotel to conduct business in this city? How many times had he brought his latest fling to his hotel suite for some after-hours pleasures, not giving a thought to them the next day, or even the hotel staff's opinion? Now he was here on a wholly different mission—one he never thought he would experience. Apprehension mixed with excitement pulsed through his veins while he made his way to the concierge desk, wheeling his suitcase behind him. A few people stopped chatting to stare at him in his jeans and brown bomber jacket as he passed by. He was hard not to look at. His roguishly good looks and tall demeanor gave him an air of authority and confidence.

The scent of the lobby was pleasant, almost intoxicating. It reminded Marcus of *her*. Earthy, floral with a hint of spice. His blood ran quicker at the prospect of seeing Simran again. How many weeks had it been? How many months? God, he was such a fucking idiot to let her go. It was selfish to think that he could just walk away from someone so amazingly real, and now expect to see her again. This was karma's way of telling him that life was a bitch, but he was well aware of that. He'd lived most of his adult life only for his own pleasures. Now, here he was trying to grasp something that, idiotically, he thought he could put behind him; something he knew even a few months ago was so good for him.

Although, he'd like to think that it wasn't his fault entirely. He'd met with unexpected issues in the launch of his new nightclub in Vancouver, and his investors got spooked. A lot of wining, dining, and hand holding had to happen to smooth things over and get them back on the road to success. Admittedly, the stress and anxiety overtook him. But, damn, there wasn't one day she didn't make it into his thoughts. Her lush smile, warm spirit, and curvy body, those were just a few things in an endless list he couldn't get off his mind. Acting like the bastard he knew he could be, he'd asked her for space between them to focus on work. When really, deep down, he'd needed to put the brakes on his strong feelings for her. She'd hated him because of it then, and really, could he blame her? But he wondered if she still hated him now.

He swiped his phone to an out-of-the blue text message from her marked 'sent' from two weeks ago. He re-read it for the hundredth time.

"Hi, Marcus, it's Simran. Everything is on track. We've met your drop-dead dates with flying colors and are targeted to launch on time. Hope to catch you to finalize everything and I can turn over your keys and other materials. If not, no worries. I'll messenger everything to you when you're back in town. Talk soon."

The message had been to the point, lacking any emotion. She was referring to his philanthropic art gallery venture. A project dedicated to helping struggling artists and something she offered to help him with while he was out of town—before they broke it off. He knew it was a huge endeavor for her to take on, especially with her workload, but she'd been excited to manage it at the time—both the mission and her feelings for him being strong motivators. Did she still care for him? Or had he completely screwed it up?

The communication from her was next to nothing before that message. The way they left things had been worse than ugly and her own work consumed her. He'd tried numerous times to reach her between their last phone conversation and this unexpected text, but she ignored him. No doubt she was still upset, but was something else going on? Had she moved on? His gut twisted. She was the real deal, so it shouldn't come as a shock if she had. But, what the hell happened?

Clearing his head, he walked to the concierge. Just as he came up, he noticed the retreating figure of a woman. A crisp, white shirt draped her shoulders and her black, loosely curled hair hit just below her shoulder blades. She disappeared behind the long marble counter, walking to the back of the lobby. The over-the-top lush greenery on the counter obscured his vision, but he tried to keep his eyes on her while she stepped onto the escalators and went up to the mirrored elevator banks. Something about the way she moved made him think of Simran. Like a dancer, the woman swayed gracefully and with intention.

A loud "ahem," interrupted his thoughts. When he looked back at the desk, he met familiar dark-chocolate-colored eyes so like Simran's his breath hitched. They were framed by clear, cat-eye shaped glasses, though, sitting on a face so similar to the one he thought about daily. Coppery, light brown skin smoothed over high cheekbones, but that's where the likeness ended, he realized on closer inspection. This woman's features were longer, her chin pointier. At a few inches taller than Simran, she was just able to manage looking down her nose at him in her heels. That familiar black, wavy hair was cut in a blunt, chin length bob. He noticed the pinched look on her face as her eyes travelled up and down his form. The look grew even more severe when she saw he recognized who she was. He didn't know her personally but knew about her.

Putting on the most charming smile he could manage in the face of such coldness (he'd met with some of the most repulsive nightclub clientele in the past for Christ's sake), he faced off with Simran's older sister. He extended a hand to her. "You must be Sabine. I've heard so much about you from Simran." She smiled back frostily, shaking his hand curtly, and he noticed hers was slender and cool, just like her sister's. Then she jerked away like she'd been burned. She straightened her red, impeccably tailored suit jacket; the pin on her lapel reading "Head of Guest Affairs" glinting gold at the sharp gesture.

"Welcome back to The Plaza, Mr. Lehigh," she said, her voice not quite as throaty as Simran's. She sniffed, "I hope your travels here were safe and pleasant. As requested, the Hagoromo private dining room has been reserved for you and your guest. We took the liberty of keeping it for you all day since you're such a valued client. In addition, the chef has planned a delicious eight course meal, complete with our best champagne, sake, freshest fish omakase, and other delights. I hope everything is to your liking." Her gaze was expectant, her dark eyes trying to drill a hole into him. He'd been to The Plaza more times than he could count for business and pleasure. He'd been taken care of with the utmost respect and discretion and had never taken notice of Sabine Khan until he'd met Simran. He was surprised to learn she was Head of Guest Affairs. She must have been the one to ensure he was well taken care of with the privacy he requested in the past. Yes, selfish didn't come close to how he viewed his former self.

"Thank you, Sabine, for taking care of all of that. And Chef English never fails when it comes to exquisite global cuisine," Marcus said with a smile. No matter how Sabine treated him, he wasn't going to play her game. "I believe I'm in my regular suite, The Fitzgerald?" he asked, referring to one of the best two-story penthouse suites on the hotel's twentieth floor.

"Of course. I can have someone take your bag up if you like," she sniffed with an arched eyebrow.

"No, I've got it, thank you."

"Have a pleasant stay," she murmured, sliding over his key card. He thanked her again and went to the escalators. He had about an hour and a half before he met with Simran. He would

freshen up in his room and take some time to think about
what he would say to her.

જ⁊જ⁊

Simran took a deep and shaky breath, exhaling forcefully,
in hopes that some negativity would exit her body. She went
to the sink and re-drenched the hand towel in cold water.
Ringing it out, she went back to the bed in her suite at The
Plaza. She laid down, then put the cool cloth on her forehead.
The worry lines started to relax. To say she was overheated
would be an understatement. The unfamiliar hormones
coursing through her at that moment, were having a field day
with her body. The chilled towel was only slightly helping;
what she needed was to stick her head in a bucket full of ice.
But the ministration of cool towel to hot forehead reminded
her so much of her mother's soothing touches when she was a
child and sick that Simran felt comforted.

Surgery had been four days ago, and recovery was a bitch.
Her abdomen pinched in several spots where the stitches held
her flesh together. Her lower back ached, and she was having
a tough time moving, not to mention the constant flux of her
internal temperature. Looking at the clock, she saw it was
close to three hours before she could take her next dose of
pain-killers.

Damn it.

"Fuck, Marcus," she said aloud. The words coming out
absent of any feeling, as she believed that anything she felt
toward him had faded after his behavior with her. Oh, but

she'd been dumb, hadn't she? This was partially her fault, wasn't it? Having been warned on numerous occasions about his reputation when they started their whirl-wind affair five months ago, she still jumped in head first. Everyone said Marcus Lehigh was a player. The brilliant global night club entrepreneur, at thirty-seven-years old was an absolute stud of a man. Unbelievably attractive and charming, he had all the world, mainly beautiful women, at his feet. It started out as just the most incredible sex between the two of them, but then quickly evolved into something else. Simran thought that maybe, just maybe, as naïve as it was to even think it, he would have changed for her. She wasn't a complete romantic; her heart having been butchered and left for dead a few years ago. But their time together felt like more than just pure attraction and lust. It had no label, she could admit that, but did they need a label when things felt so right between them?

She closed her eyes to the vivid memory of when they first met. She was punishing herself with these thoughts, a masochist torturing herself mentally because everything from the chemistry to the banter had felt perfect. How could she ever forget it? The animal magnetism was so heavy between them, just hanging in the air. You could see it, smell its headiness like a sex driven magic spell if you concentrated hard enough. Even now, her own body felt the familiar heaviness in her breasts shifting down to her pelvis, as she recalled that time.

Five Months Ago,
London

२

Chapter 2

Simran was on a much-needed vacation from an insane, work fueled life in New York City. She chose her two weeks of free time to visit her childhood friend, Bettina, in London. She and Bettina had known each other since they were young girls, their families having met years ago within the well-to-do South Asian community in Greenwich, CT. The two round-faced Indian girls, aged eight, connected immediately over a game of hopscotch and the Harry Potter book series (both of them secretly agreeing that Malfoy was a cutie, even though he was not a good boy). Having ended up at the same all girls private school, they never looked back. Tina, as her close friends called her, was the yang to Simran's yin, two dynamic personalities complementing one another. While Tina was care-free and charismatic, Simran was more serious and internal. She'd been that way since her mother died of stomach cancer the previous year in India, before moving to Connecticut with her sister. With Tina's help throughout the years, she came out of her shell and found her sense of humor again. Both women, with the support of one another, grew into attractive, smart, and dynamic individuals.

After they both graduated from NYU, their paths deviated. Simran chose a career in events planning, pushing herself to early success, while also obtaining her MBA from the Stern School of Business. Tina floundered after graduation, trying a few career paths. First Public Relations (too many parties to focus), then Marketing (too many numbers involved in the Profit and Loss statements), and even making a go at Events Planning (too much organization required). She just didn't have the attention for any of it. So, two years ago, at the age of thirty, Tina decided to explore the marriage her parents wanted to arrange for her. This came as a total shock to everybody. She was known to strongly poo-poo arranged marriages, touting herself as a modern Indian woman.

"A modern Indian woman can be with the times and still get a little help from her parents, can't she?" she'd argued to her friends, and emphatically to Simran. Simran knew better than anyone that this could be true, her father having supported her financially through her college years and master's degree (and because he never let her forget it). She, along with everyone else, said if Tina was happy, then they were happy for her, and to hell with the gossip mongers in their Indian community who found anything to wag their tongues about.

Tina's prospective fiancé, Raj Kunil, was handsome and quiet. His family prospered in the South Asian textile industry and claimed a royal lineage. Having studied finance at Cambridge University, he was now working for a London high stakes hedge fund. Their courtship had been a year of back and forth between England and NYC, facilitated by a close family friend who was also a well-respected match-maker in their circle. Although Tina and Raj's personalities were on opposite spectrums, they seemed to complement one another. Their wedding was a huge affair in India filled with seven hundred of their closest friends and relatives (and that was the edited down guest list). As far as arranged marriages went, theirs ended up as a match made in heaven. They were two really good-looking South Asians from well-to-do families. Both harbored a love of travel, life's pleasure, and a mutual agreement on the benefits of their marriage (the joining of their same, social standing families in a time-honored tradition). And to cap it all off, the two actually liked and enjoyed each other's company! No one could ask for a better arrangement.

❧❦❧❦❧

Friday night in London. It was early spring and there was still a bit of a chill left in the air. Tina arranged a limousine for their group of six girlfriends, including Simran, to take them from one hot club to another for a night out on the town. All were dressed up in their snazziest, most expensive, and sexiest ensembles. Their plans included starting off with a hot new club opening which Raj was able to snag tickets for. The perks of having a client who was also an investor in the club. Raj was working late but would meet them later. And to Simran's exasperation, also bringing along a friend Tina was sure could give Simran the much-needed boning she deserved. She didn't want to think about how she'd probably regressed back to a virgin with her lack of sexual partners in the last year.

They arrived at Club Liberated in the artsy neighborhood of Bermondsey filled with awe and excitement. The place was incredible with a capital "I." As a successful events planner in her own right, and one who harbored a love for architecture and style, Simran knew a thing or two about interior design. The aesthetics of this club were distinct in upcoming interior trends, flowing seamlessly together without being obnoxious. The layout was huge and open, with different sections partitioned off in intricate, almost Moghul-style floor to ceiling woodwork which were painted in a black lacquer finish. A large dance floor made up one area, where the DJ thumped dance music that wasn't annoyingly garish; DJ Krush's hypnotic beats currently on rotation. There was a deep stage for live acts in the next space over, with a crowded audience already there. Sexy contortionists were the evening's feature and they stopped to watch them for a bit, too, wowed by their talents. The dancers in racy burlesque wear, displayed their supple skills worthy of any Cirque du Soleil type show. In yet another part, a masculine lounge area beckoned with a warm glow coming from the artistic Edison bulb lighting installations. Club goers were splayed on the tan, leather loungers that completed the intimate area. At the center of the entire large expanse, though, was the focal point that really grabbed Simran's attention. Lit up in soft and sexy electric blue lighting which bounced off the mirrors behind the liquor bottles, was a large circle bar; a half a dozen or so bartenders were busy mixing and serving the sophisticated clientele who were swarming about. The bar catered to all of the club areas, standing underneath an expanse of skylights with thousands of strings beaded in diamond-like crystals hanging down. There were so many that they all came together to look like one massive shimmering body that swayed gently, almost erotically, every so often. The whole thing created a fantastically magical effect which made Simran stop in her tracks, mesmerized. She didn't have a chance to explore more because Tina and her entourage met up with more friends. They went over to their reserved tables near both the circle bar and the dance floor.

"Let's get this party started!" Tina hollered to the group, as they slid into the plush purple booths. The soft blue from the bar bounced a violet hue off of everyone and everything. Socializing got underway with bottle service flowing and everyone chatting at once.

By far, Simran was the most popular that night amongst the large group of about twenty South Asians. The feisty New Yorker, as she came to be known by the crowd of *Desis* (those of the Indian subcontinent who live abroad), made her rounds to the different clusters, cracking jokes. This was her go to approach when she was out and about with people she barely knew, and it went over well. She said something naughty about Aunties (a phrase for older South Asian women who "meant well" with their judgmental gossip) in miniskirts and another round of laughter erupted around her. She threw her head back with a throaty laugh, too. Her naturally wavy, black hair floated down to rest on her back, gliding along the intricate draping of her silver mesh top. She felt so alive and grateful to be with Tina and her crew. The past year had been a non-stop whirling dervish of events and continuing the growth of her business, *Lavish Your Events*. She'd finally managed to pull in some higher net worth clients whom she'd been courting for the past two years. She absolutely deserved this chance to let loose and celebrate, and she knew her best friend was *the* person for this.

Something in her peripheral made her glance at the bar and that's when she noticed him. He was leaning casually against a barstool, facing away from the bar, a drink cradled in his hands. His focus was in their direction. Some judgmental dude, gawking at the *Desis'* raucous behavior, probably thinking they needed to tone it down a notch. She'd seen it before. Sometimes her friends' and family's festive mood could get out of hand, and at times, she became irritated, too. But right now, she wanted to rejoice in her accomplishments, go a little wild, and this was how celebrating was meant to be, unabashedly loud, and a little nutty. She wasn't too surprised, but annoyance simmered in her. This was a club for Pete's sake and they *had* reserved the space. She turned her head for a better view and saw he was extremely attractive, and instead of a reproachful look, he was staring straight at her intensely, a half grin on his super handsome face. The look he gave her was magnetic, trying to pull her in. Even from where she stood, she noticed his eyes, so bright, so commanding. Something warm unfurled in her chest and dropped heavily to her stomach. It was desire, a familiar dormant friend returning in full force. She looked away, thinking she'd made a mistake, then snuck a look back again. His half grin was still there, and he cocked an eyebrow in her direction. WHAT A FOX.

He mouthed, "Hi," to her, and she swore she got a little moist in her panties at the innocently suggestive gesture. All she could think to do was give him a saucy half smile and turn away. She hadn't played the field in forever and she was more than rusty. The thing was, she *was* on vacation, and it could be fun, but did she want to go there?

A server came up, offering her a drink. "From the gentleman at the bar," they said. It was what she was currently drinking, a Belvedere vodka martini on the rocks with a lemon twist. Surprised, she took the fresh drink and turned back to the man. She air toasted him and took a sip. Then headed back to her group.

Chapter 3

That evening, Marcus didn't have any expectations for their club launch party, except it would go off without a hitch. Tickets were sold out and he knew they had a success on their hands. He was one of the best at what he did, and in the past twelve years since starting *LC Enterprises & Holdings*, a Global Entertainment Company, he was confident in what he and his business partner were doing. His humble beginnings right out of college involved helping a family friend overhaul their flailing supper club in Santa Barbara, which led to more fruitful opportunities. Eventually, he roped his friend into opening their own night club, and then the company. At this point in his career, with five well known global establishments and a dozen more successful partnerships under their belts, Marcus was flying high. Or should have been.

Tonight's opening night felt more like an after-thought considering all the work he'd put into making sure the venue ran like clockwork and went above his customer base's expectations. Marcus was here to ensure their GM was on point with operations, and to show face for the routine protocol of a few press interviews. Then he planned to head home and relax in peace. Their Publicity team could handle the flock of social media personalities, and other special guests, who waltzed through with complimentary invitations in hand looking for a good time and other freebies. All necessary to help elevate the place by influencer word of mouth, social media content, and high ratings, but absolutely out of his tolerance to deal with.

Before Marcus could relax though, he also had to ensure his business partner stayed out of trouble. He was honestly more confident about the launch party than in Bruce. The guy *really* enjoyed all the perks of this business a little too much, even after a decade of playing hard. His score card of women and crazy escapades put Marcus' own "extra-curricular" activities to shame. This was saying a lot considering Marcus was recognized as a global playboy amongst their own social circles. Not that the bad press hurt too much in their industry; any press was good press for them when it came to a player's lifestyle, but only to a certain degree. There were times when Bruce took it a bit too far. Marcus was always there to help him out, always would be, because they were close, having been friends since college.

Actually, there was a period when Marcus had participated in the wild ride, too, hopping from woman to woman, jumping from continent to continent without a care in the world. In the last few years, however, he'd made his sexual pursuits (still persistent in his life) more of a discretion. After having a private affair leaked to the press and someone dear to him getting hurt, he now kept things under-wraps, not wanting to get too personal with his flings.

More recently, he'd had a restless feeling that he couldn't shake. It began when they'd started the initial plans for Club

Liberated two years ago. Now it was settled in like an old and comfortable companion. Was he having a mid-life crisis? At thirty-seven it wasn't out of the question. But he already had the jet-setting lifestyle, had all the women he could ever screw; hell, he had all the fast and fancy sports cars he could race until he crashed and burned, so what was eating him? Not sure what to do about it, he'd started working on auto-pilot. He continued to refine their clubs' day-to-day operations with management and oversee an ever-growing portfolio. He still entertained a slew of women, usually not having to try too hard in that department because they came to him. But it was all becoming mind-numbing. The only thing offering any hint of true enjoyment was a new initiative they started for up-and-coming artists. Marcus was the brains behind it, wanting to offer local creators the opportunity to showcase their work at *LC Enterprises'* venues. It was a way for talent to get their art to the public, including live acts and musical performers. But other than that, the days were a blur. Maybe he needed to pick up a new hobby or find something completely new to keep him fulfilled.

Hearing the boisterous laughter from the group nearest the bar had caught his attention that night, especially the striking woman with the long, black hair. *Now there was a suitable distraction.* He'd caught her eye and mouthed a greeting to her, and in return, she'd smiled coyly back at him. After sending a drink refresher over, he'd fully expected her to come to him. Instead, she acknowledged him from afar, then went back to her friends. *Cheeky.*

Marcus couldn't remember the last time a woman hadn't come to his beck and call immediately. People knew who he was around this city, and he usually didn't have to wait for an introduction. This gorgeous woman had him waiting and he was more intrigued than annoyed. This was going to be fun. It had been a *long* time since he'd chased some tail.

He'd been glancing over at her and her fashionable group of friends for the past half hour now. How could he not? They were a large and lively crowd. The woman in question was flitting from table-to-table, conversing, and making jokes; the laughter erupting wherever she went. He chuckled when he saw her dart and artfully spin away from the men who tried to pull her onto their laps. Undoubtedly, she had a hell of a sense of humor and, damn, what a sexy laugh; he could hear it from here, low and husky. He found both of those not only refreshing but instantly arousing. Her body language was lithe and supple, breaking into movement every so often to the music the DJ spun. She was probably unaware that she was even doing it, and his glance couldn't help but stray to her every time she did. There was an attraction there that made the blood pump faster in his veins; an animalistic reaction to hunt something, or someone.

He didn't realize he was wearing a silly half grin until he turned around to order her a fresh drink and caught sight of himself in the mirrors. He wanted to get to know her. Any red-blooded man would. Lush, black hair floated toward her nicely formed ass encased in tiny, dark shorts. The club lights danced along the coppery skin of her shoulders and shapely calves, and the slinky top she wore only accentuated her full curves. He wanted to be that slinky top, and his mouth involuntarily watered thinking about getting acquainted with those curves *much* better. Awash in the hazy violet hue, jewels on both her dangerously high heels and a clip sweeping one side of her hair back caught the light, twinkling like tiny starbursts. And that face, damn. From where he was, he could make out high cheekbones in a soft face with a slightly pointed chin. Would she be a stubborn thing in bed, or would she be yielding, letting him take all the control? He noticed her mouth then. Sensual and red, those full lips were open in laughter, and his thoughts went dirtier on how she could make good use of those lips. He took a long sip of his drink to calm down his libido and the growing snugness in his pants.

৩৩৩৩

Seriously, what could it hurt? She *was* on vacation and maybe this could be the tasty cherry on top of the fantastic time she was already having. And speaking of cherries, maybe he could help her pop the one that had probably re-grown back in her nether regions.

Simran made her way over to where Tina was holding court in the round corner booth. Whispering that she was heading to the bar, she nodded her head in the foxy man's direction. Tina looked over, turned back to Simran with an excited grin, and gave her two enthusiastic thumbs up.

She squared her shoulders and sauntered up to him, her legs shaking slightly with both anticipation and nervousness. Up close, he was not only roguishly handsome, but had an amazing physique. *Oh, good God, yes.* A white, button-down shirt was tucked into perfectly tailored, cobalt blue suit pants, which encased his long legs. The matching suit jacket he wore outlined broad shoulders, and accentuated solid arm muscles. With no tie, his collar opened a few buttons down along a tan neck, and she could see a hint of curly hair on his chest. Tousled dark and light blond met together in thick locks covering his head. He stood up when she approached and he was tall, towering inches over six feet which suited her five foot, seven inches perfectly. In her heels, she could just meet his lips with only slight difficulties—if it went in that direction that is. He was unquestionably a hunky, tall drink of water, and she was thirsty.

"So, to whom do I thank for my delicious drink refresher?" she asked as she set her glass down on the bar next to him, peeping up at him from under lashes. She didn't want to seem too obvious.

"I'm Marcus Lehigh," he said, in the wake of a sexy chuckle. His voice came out low and gravelly, making her shiver. The look he gave her was expectant with a thick eyebrow raised and a small smile playing around his amazing lips. And holy wow, those eyes up close. They were a piercing ice blue, the light color a discerning contrast to his tan skin. They bore into her with a heat that made her toes curl while he waited for a response.

Simran was taken aback. Not only was his accent American but there was an expectation that she should know who he was. He put out his right hand, large and inviting. Taking it, she felt warmth spread up her arm as he slowly shook, and he didn't immediately let go. His thumb ran lightly over her palm, making her almost purr in delight at the sensation. *Jeez.* This kind of human contact from a man like him was going to render her brain non-functioning, allowing the rest of her body parts to take over. *Maybe that was a good thing...?*

She cocked her head, squinting up at him, and tried to place his name. Had she heard of him before? Fresh mint and musk filled her nostrils then, and she got a little dizzy, her head cloudy. God, what a sexy combination. It took all her restraint not to lean into him and take a nice, long whiff. She noticed his pupils dilated as his eyes roved up and down her body, causing her nether regions to clench in impatience. *Down, girl!*

Studying him a little closer, she more than liked what she saw. He wasn't just handsome, he was beautiful. A sharp jawline outlined his square chin, with a slight dimple embedded in the center. His nose was long and straight, but with a bit of an upturn to the end of it. No man should have a nose like that. It was like a snub nose, but absolutely masculine and delicious on him. Then, he smiled wider at her confusion and deep dimples appeared around his mouth with crinkles around those beautiful eyes. She found it hard to breath, her lungs rendered incapacitated when only shallow bursts of air managed to exhale out. How could such a man exist? Women *and* men, hell, even animals must trip over themselves to be around him.

8

Chapter 4

er husky voice made Marcus' dick perk up further, and he discreetly shifted his pants as she turned to him, putting her drink down. He stared at her deeply again. She was even more stunning up close. Those eyes of hers, so big, dark, and almond shaped; he could get lost in those eyes, a cliché he always thought was boloney up until now. He noticed her elegant nose had a very slight curve to it, and there was a beauty spot right above her bow shaped lips, on her left side. He wanted to lick that little spot, no, he *needed* to lick that little spot. He realized, after a beat, while still holding her cool hand, that she didn't know who he was. Oh, he was most definitely in it to win it.

"I'm really happy to see guests enjoying themselves in my newest club." He nodded his head toward her friends' direction.

Letting out a noise that sounded almost like a disbelieving guffaw, she turned her back to the bar, resting her elbows on the surface. Marcus almost let out a groan of appreciation. Her curves were on full display, and he couldn't help resting his eyes on those high, full breasts, draped in the cool, silver mesh of her top. She glanced at him and smirked. *Busted!*

Although, truthfully, he wasn't doing a very good job of *not* ogling her and she didn't seem to mind.

"You're the owner of this club? Wow," she breathed. "I'm not in this business per se … I'm an events planner. But I can appreciate what you've done with the design. It's well thought out and beautiful," she said with honesty. "It would make a great venue for a large wedding party," she continued, lost in thoughtful wonder, her large eyes keenly looking around. She gazed up to the night sky through the skylights and to the iridescent crystal beads, shimmering from the pumped in cool air. Marcus' eyes flickered up, too. There was an ethereal quality to the sparkling strings against the dark sky; the exact captivating experience he'd been shooting for when he worked with their designer. It was almost heart-stopping but freeing at the same time; a perfect nod to Club Liberated's theme. When he glanced back down to her, he felt light, and he noticed the crystals making playful patterns on her face and exposed neck. How would her skin taste if he kissed her neck, sucked that soft, vulnerable spot where her pulse beat? He reeled his mind back trying to concentrate on what she just said.

"Thank you," he replied, his brows furrowed and a faint smile on his lips, pleasantly surprised. He could tell she wasn't bullshitting him and while he appreciated her praise, he was a little caught off guard. He was even more curious about this woman now. "I'm not the sole owner, there were a few of us involved, but I did manage a lot of the design details firsthand. I enjoy that kind of work." As he spoke, he noticed Bruce and his entourage of three females leaving the roped off VIP lounge. They stopped by to say hello; the leggy women giggling as they met up with Marcus. "Hey! Everyone enjoying themselves?" he asked as he shook hands with Bruce, patting him on the back. "How was it in there, Bruce, service run smoothly?"

"Absolutely fucking perfect, Marc," Bruce said, grinning, as he turned to a woman on each arm to confirm. "Right, ladies?" All of the leggy ladies tittered and agreed, but the third one, not on Bruce's arm, sidled up to Marcus and he automatically put his arm around her waist.

"Couldn't be any better, Mr. Lehigh," she cooed as she looked up with doe-eyes. He smirked in return, telling her to call him Marcus.

ↀↀↀ

Simran rolled her eyes starting to lose interest because of the flirty interaction between Marcus and the woman. The long-limbed creature was practically climbing his tall figure in her micro mini skirt which barely covered her behind. *Gross.* This was so not her scene. She was definitely dealing with a player here, and honestly what did she expect? She was in a glamorous nightclub, trying to converse with one of the owners who oozed a confident sexuality about him; one who seemed more than happy to have numerous women vying for his attention. And, if she was truly being honest with herself, she wished she'd moved quicker so that she was the one climbing his tall figure, but that wasn't how she did things.

She cocked her head, studying the pretty people mingling in front of her, and realized that she must've been a very fleeting encounter, one easily forgotten when faced with an over-eager woman. Oddly, this scenario felt a little akin to some of her awkward, junior high experiences during co-ed dances. Some of her crushes (young, white adolescent boys in her suburban Connecticut town) would spend most of the evening hanging and goofing off with her. But when the slow songs came on, they chose another girl to dance with, leaving Simran standing in the peripheral to watch. The "preferred" dance partners were usually those who fit a certain comfort zone (i.e., *not* a brown girl with a very different cultural background). She came to grasp, as she grew into a teen, and then a young woman, becoming more comfortable in her own skin, that these boys hadn't possessed the self-assurance to show they were into someone who wasn't like them. Not their fault completely, but still stupid boys. Of course, she was past that now (mostly) and knew her own self-worth. She wasn't about to play second fiddle here—to a twat and a full grown-man who should know better—even though she'd felt a physical connection like she'd never felt before with this guy. Maybe the dude Raj brought later would do, even if he only had a fraction of the swoon-worthy attributes this Marcus Lehigh possessed. She flicked her hair over a shoulder, moving away from the bar without a backward glance. She didn't get far. Marcus jumped to attention, letting go of 'micro mini skirt,' and maneuvering his tall frame quickly into her path so that she almost ran into the solid wall of his chest. She blinked in surprise at his hint of chest hair, and his all-consuming scent. *What is happening?*

"Bruce Canyon, my partner in this venture," he introduced his friend to her. "Bruce, this is ..." he trailed off, grazing his hand against the small of her back, as if urging her to stay.

"Simran Khan," she blurted out in a gasp, shocked at the electricity-like fission where his hand lay. Was he feeling this, too? She glanced quickly up to him, his eyes fixated only on her, and they were so bright, so sexy, that she had to look away. She flashed a smile in Bruce's direction, trying to overcome the trippy sensation she was experiencing with the foxy man. Bruce, apparently the more open player of the two, immediately focused his attention on her, the three women with him momentarily forgotten.

"*Simran,*" Bruce said smoothly, "I hope you're enjoying yourself." He took her hand in his, bringing it to his lips, his green eyes giving her a rascally look, while thick black locks fell over his forehead. *Whoa, so gorgeous, too,* Simran thought, and started to get a little flustered. She felt Marcus' hand slightly tighten on her back.

"Bruce, why don't you take these ladies over to view the dancers on stage?" Marcus growled a little too vehemently at his friend, before she could even start to answer. "Ladies," he said pleasantly, and with a dismissal, he turned his back on them to focus on her. "So, Simran, is it?"

"Yes," she said, the sound of her name rolling off his tongue so smooth, like liquid chocolate she wanted to roll her entire body in. "We didn't get that far did we?" she laughed. He chuckled with her, and the low timbre was so masculine she wanted to melt into him. "You know you can go with them if you want," she nodded toward the retreating group. "Don't let me keep you from your, uh festivities," she said a little too prickly, her shoulders shrugging. *Calm down, you freak. You just met him.*

She heard his deep chuckle again, and her cheeks heated in embarrassment, as she toyed with the lemon slice in her drink and took a bite, thoughtfully chewing the sour, alcohol drenched fruit.

"The only party I'm interested in tonight is right here," he said, and Simran raised an eyebrow at him as he winked. "So, does your name mean anything?" he continued curiously.

Really? This old hat? "It does actually. It means 'remembrance.'" He nodded. Was he actually interested in her name, or was this his way of trying to get into her panties? She waited for the smart-ass remark, trying to link the meaning of her name with a night to remember.

"I did some work in India, opened a club there with Bruce. But in all the time I spent there, I never met a Simran before. It's a beautiful name, suits you perfectly." His tone was candid as those bright eyes raked over her again. Simran was momentarily speechless. *Who is this guy?*

"So, events planning?" he continued, focusing back on their previous conversation, and taking a sip of his drink. "Hmm, I may be in need of your services sometime soon." He paused, stroking his dimpled chin while giving her a thoughtful look. She could almost see the gears shifting in his head while he considered her for a moment, his eyes slit.

Simran arched her brows doubtfully. They were going to talk about work? *Ok.* If she couldn't make physical contact, she could at least claim another client. She leaned her elbow on the bar, putting her chin in her hand, and pasted on a fake smile. Inwardly she groaned, so not prepared for this conversation. *Was foxy man turning out to be a dud?*

Then he spoke, ready to reveal his plan. "Picture this: *you*, Simran, help *me* create an event; an experience if you will. Let's see," he continued to stroke his chin, obviously putting some real thought into his words. "We can start off by slowly building momentum; maybe offer some scintillating activities first, a teaser for what's to come." His eyelids lowered slightly, and he stepped closer to her. "But we'll definitely take the time to hint at the gratification that we'll end with." He paused, looking her up and down again, and Simran was positive he was undressing her with his eyes. Goosebumps budded up all over her exposed skin. He gave her a wink again, then he went on, his voice soft. "When momentum has hit its peak, we'll deliver an unstoppable, mind-blowing experience, multiple times, I can absolutely assure you." His tone was exuding confidence bordering on arrogance, and now, Simran couldn't turn away, even if she wanted to. Arrogance in a man was her Achilles heel. "The pleasure will be loud and wild, probably heard from any given rooftop." He shrugged, turning to take a sip of his drink again. "I have a feeling the reviews will be top-notch." That last part was finished with a wicked grin, his white teeth against his tan skin making him absolutely wolfish. He was close enough for her to feel the warmth emanating from his broad chest and her nipples pebbled up to say 'hello.' *Nope, definitely the opposite of a dud.*

Her brain was mush now. A hot guy will do that to a horny woman. She stood up straighter, tossing her hair over her shoulder while her brain worked overtime trying to grasp at what he was going on about. *He can't seriously be talking Marketing 101 right now.* When the words finally sank in, Simran gave an unladylike snort, and she had to cover her mouth before her nervous giggles burst out. Did that shit really work on women? She glanced up and saw he was laughing, too, but the lust in his eyes was unmistakable. Those goosebumps from before? Well now they rippled down, disappearing into her satin shorts and underwear. There was no denying the dampness between her legs now. She knew she wanted to see where this would go and would happily let him into her panties.

"Hold on," she said, still trying to hide her giggles. He was definitely a smooth charmer in an unexpected way. "Before I even consider helping you with this mind-blowing experience, shouldn't we get to know one another a little better?" She eyed him and that delectable dimple in his chin. She wanted to finger it so badly. "You know, it goes against my work ethic if I don't know the entire picture," she countered with a hand up, her tone taking a mock seriousness, and her eyes wide.

"You're absolutely right," Marcus said, his bright eyes twinkling now. *How did one not get lost in them?* She felt him softly caressing the knuckles of her hand midair and Simran both heard and felt blood whoosh in her ears. "Why don't you tell me about yourself. You aren't from London are you?" He was referring to her own American accent.

"Nope. I'm a New Yorker. I'm visiting an old friend here." And she tilted her chin in Tina's direction. She explained she was here for two weeks on a much-needed break from her hectic life as sole owner of a successful boutique events planning company. She learned he was from the US, too, Santa Barbara, CA, to be exact, but didn't really have one home. He was so busy with club openings and other ventures, that he acquired a few condos around the world. In London, however, he was living on his yacht.

෪෪෪

"*Oh*, just your yacht. Got it. That must be downright *awful*," she teased and laughed. Marcus joined in her throaty laughter, actually enjoying that she wasn't impressed with his lifestyle. It was refreshing and different from the fawning women he was so used to.

"All right, I'm hearing it out loud, and I must sound so full of myself. Honestly, though, why settle down in one place when there's so much to experience in the world," and as he said this, he rested his hand lightly on the small of her back again, feeling that same warm connection as before, while he made small circles right above her ass cheeks. Her back arched slightly, and he heard a very, very soft moan. *Fuck, she's hot.* It took all of his own strength to not glide down all the way and squeeze. "I'll settle down someday, just haven't found the right time, or place." He paused, dropping his hand before he crossed a line they couldn't come back from, but leaned in closer to smell her scent. It was intoxicating. The combination of earthy, floral, and a touch of spice was driving him crazy and had been since she'd come up to the bar. He continued leaning in further, looking her face over again, awash in the dim light and dancing crystals. She really was lovely. He couldn't believe Bruce had tried to cock-block him back there. He'd not only seen her first, but there was something between them that he just had to see through. "You know, Simran, I'd love to show you my yacht sometime. I could help you with some of that much-needed unwinding." Her breathing came a little faster then, and her cheeks pinkened. She looked at his lips and licked her own. Was he making her nervous? Or was he pushing all her hot buttons? He hoped it was the latter.

She leaned forward, giving him a better view of her ample cleavage. Her voice came out low and husky, "I'd like that, too ... Marcus ... *if* I can fit you in." And she boldly travelled her dark eyes from his lips, down to his crotch.

Raw lust pulsed straight down to his dick, making it stiffen even more. The latter, definitely the latter. Did she say "if?" She wasn't giving in easily. And at that moment, he felt like a raging hormonal teenager. It was all he could do to not imagine burying himself in her warm, curvy body. She was licking those luscious lips again, and he had to shift once more while his pants grew tighter.

The music suddenly turned to an upbeat Daft Punk mix and Simran moved away. She cocked her head to listen while slightly wiggling her shoulders to the beat.

"This is an awesome track. I really love what the DJ is playing tonight," she commented, breaking the sexual tension, thankfully. *Yes, good, let's talk about music and I can get my hard-on to calm down,* Marcus thought. As an events planner in NYC of all places, she must know a thing or two about music. He geared himself up, ready to listen to her chat about mainstream pop or dance tunes, while he feigned some interest. Instead, she started on about the UK club scene and the evolution of underground music. As she continued to speak, enthusiastically in fact, he found his attraction not calming down. *Well, well, well.* Here was a person who had a handle on this topic and anyone who knew him closely recognized that his secret passion was music. It was his mode of escape; a way to unwind from the daily grind. Not just any music, but underground club music, drum and bass, electronica, and techno. His knowledge and love of it bordered on nerdery, or so he'd been told more than once by his buddies in college. Now, he rarely talked about it unless he was in a heated discussion with a music industry professional. He was a little speechless as Simran continued talking. Here was a sensual and smart woman, sassy, too. He had to have her, and she damn well was going to "fit him in" if he had anything to do with it. There was no denying she wanted him, too, he'd noticed the tell-tale signs.

When Usher's "Yeah" spun on, she exclaimed, "Classic!" and started moving her curvy hips, her breasts bouncing softly to the rhythm. *Damn.* He was definitely hooked. She then asked him if he wanted to dance.

"Hmm, I'm not much of a dancer, but I think I could be persuaded," he replied, eyeing her sensual body swaying to the beat of the music. Like a fish caught on a line, he followed her lead.

As they moved through the crowd, he saw Bruce and his entourage already dirty dancing amongst the mass of bodies. They'd no doubt end up back at his London condo for a night of debauchery, Marcus thought wryly. Bruce did a double take when he saw Marcus and caught his eye, giving him an incredulous guffaw then a nod in approval because Marcus never made an appearance on the dance floor. Bruce started mouthing some crude words at him regarding Simran and he shook his head, choosing to ignore the juvenile behavior and just concentrate on the hot babe dragging him out onto the floor.

Chapter 5

With his hand in hers, Simran led him to the crowd of gyrating clubgoers. She looked back over her shoulder and saw him grinning as he followed. *Sweet, baby Krishna, he's a looker.* What happened to her back there? When he asked if she wanted to see his yacht, she wanted to tell him, hell yes, I want on your yacht and more. But this was a different breed of man. A completely cocky, smooth, if not fine, specimen, who probably always got what he wanted. She knew the type; she'd been dodging men like him since her business stepped into the arena of higher net worth clients recently. What was it about money that made otherwise semi-normal and handsome men into giant, arrogant players? She'd never been interested in the type before, but something about Marcus, made her bold and she wanted to experience him. She couldn't believe she'd said she could "possibly fit him in." Her behavior was bordering on slutty and she kind of liked it.

Lifting her arms in the air, she started moving more fully, gracefully shaking her body—the music taking over her senses. She felt his hard body come up behind her, his big, warm hands grabbing her hips to pull her close, while he moved his body in pace with hers. Hmm, he had some rhythm, or maybe he had two left feet and she was so in lust for him, she didn't notice or care. The song shifted right into Flo Rida's "Right Round" and his hands slid to the front of her pelvis and jerked her hips back to his. She could feel the hardness of his length along her backside.

"Now this is my kind of song," he murmured. She smirked because of course it was. A song about a guy receiving amazing head was every man's kind of song and no doubt his wish for the night, too. "I hope you don't get motion sickness, Simran, because when I go down on you, your head will spin. You *will* remember it," Marcus said in her ear. *Oh, good lord!* There it was—his oh so clever link to her name, and her blood ran hot in her veins. She couldn't even find a suitable answer. Instead, she gyrated her backside back into him, and flexed into a body roll to tease him. It only aroused herself more. The heat building in her body started to shoot down between her legs; lava pieces spouting from a volcano before it exploded. Oh God, was she going to lose it on the dance floor?

"You're like a sexy feline." His voice was gruff now, and his breath was warm in her ear, turning her on even further. She closed her eyes to the dizzying sensation. She could smell the smoky bourbon on his breath, and she wondered what he would taste like.

"Mm," she purred back, as his hands slid up her waist. He pushed her hair aside and started nuzzling her neck, his nose gliding down her skin as she heard him inhale deeply.

"Why don't we get some air?" he suggested softly. Giggling, she breathlessly agreed. He grabbed her hand this time and led her to the patio doors. She made a quick stop to tell Tina she was heading outside. Tina only raised her stylized brows at them. Then her mouth broke into a huge smile and she waved Simran off approvingly. *She better be pleased,* Simran thought. Tina knew she was in dire need of some action and hadn't stopped trying to hook her up since she stepped off the plane.

"You have thirty minutes and we're out of here, though," Tina called a reminder to her. *Ok, bartender, make it a quickie!*

Marcus led her out to the large back deck which was artfully outfitted with potted trees, chaise lounges and twinkle lights. A relaxed bar catered to a few groups of people lounging around, chatting with drinks. The view from the patio was of the glittering city and the Thames below.

"Gorgeous," she breathed out, her breath visible in the early spring chill of the night air.

"Yes, absolutely agree," he murmured, his cool blue eyes only on her. She felt his jacket swing over her now shivering shoulders and then he immediately pulled her into his solid, warm form. She sunk into him and felt his hardness pressing into her groin. Her breath caught. It was one thing to feel it against her backside while dancing in a group of people, but he was all up in her business now, intimately so, and it felt freaking phenomenal. *Was this really happening?* Grinning, he pushed her back to a shadowed part of the deck, whispering something about discretion. Appreciative for his considerate behavior regarding privacy, she started to tell him so when all words flew out of her head as one strong arm wrapped her closer to him, and the other went to the back of her neck. His fingers threaded through her hair as his lips descended on to hers.

It wasn't a gentle kiss to start with by any means. It was passionate, a little wild, and he tasted like the expensive bourbon he'd been drinking. His mouth was demanding, moving over hers, licking, sucking, finally persuading hers to open to his. Their tongues met in a crazy tangle, with his finally sliding over sensually and hers following. She responded by moaning softly and rubbing her breasts deliciously against him. Her hands glided up the solid wall of his chest and down his muscular arms, the cool of his crisp shirt barely concealing the warmth from his skin underneath. She wanted to feel all of him against her and wrapped her arms around his waist, then up his back, the jacket falling to the ground. She didn't care; she wasn't chilly anymore. Her body was alive and on fire and this absolutely gorgeous man was hers for the moment.

When his warm hands slid slowly down her back, her breath hitched again. Never had she so willingly let a man handle her like this after having just met. But this particular man was driving her senseless and she needed his hands on her. He reached her ass and gave a squeeze. "What I would love to do to this perfect, round ass," he growled against her as he nipped his way down her neck. She felt his teeth and lips pulling at the base of her neck and she whimpered low, gyrating against his solid length, rubbing herself into a frenzy. She panted at her own wanton behavior, and how good it felt. He growled again against her shoulder, and his hand slowly went up the front of her waist, almost as if giving her the choice to stop him. She arched her back, offering her breasts, and he continued, palming one, squeezing, and rubbing his

thumb over her already hardened nipple. She felt and heard
the low hum of appreciation come from him, only making her
body bow further, pressing her hips further to his. "Easy,
kitten," he whispered against her ear, then pushed her back
again until her back met the wall. He grasped her thigh and
pulled her leg around him, opening her heat to him fully. "Holy
hell. You're so hot, kitten. I'm going to have to fuck you all
night," he warned against her lips. All she could do was nod
and breath a 'yes you will' in response to his dirty words. God,
how she wanted this bad. She wanted *him* bad.

❧❧❧❧

"Simran? *Oh,* Sima? You out here? It's time to jet." The
quiet of their heated make out session was interrupted
abruptly by her friend's loud voice and The Weeknd's
"Starboy" blaring from inside the club. Their private bubble
had burst. He felt her reluctantly pull away from him,
confusion on her face as she looked over his shoulder.

"*Come on*, Sima, on to the next stop! You've been out here
for almost a half hour. I'm in charge tonight, remember?" her
friend continued as she stood in the club doorway, holding the
door open, one hand on a jutting out hip. She was ready to
leave with her fur stole slung over one shoulder and artfully
down her form-fitting jumpsuit. She squinted around, finally
spotting them in the shadowed corner and called back, "Ok,
lady, I'm giving you five more minutes but the limo is waiting.
Meet you out front, ok?" And she went back inside, tottering a
little in her sky-high, silver heels.

Marcus let out a low whistle as he caught his breath. Christ, he had to cool off. This woman was absolutely intoxicating. Her friend interrupting had to be a good thing because they might have had sex right here on the deck of his new nightclub if she hadn't. Mind-blowing sex, without a question, but not his thing. Discretion was his number one rule when it came to his personal pursuits. He looked down at Simran trying to catch her own breath and fuck if he wouldn't throw out his rulebook for more time with her. Her uneven breathing came out of swollen lips, and pink bloomed her cheeks. Her top was askew, further exposing the top mounds of those luscious breasts, with the hint of a lacy, bright fuchsia bra peeping out. He wanted to rip both of them off of her completely. Instead, he brushed his hand against her to move her top back into place. She gasped and looked up at him, her dark-chocolate eyes turned black with desire. He could see the raw need in them, and damn, he wanted to finish what they started.

He bent down to retrieve his jacket and while doing so, stopped to crouch in front of her. On his haunches, his hands came up to caress the petal softness on the back of her knees.

"*Oh*," she exhaled, clutching his shoulders while her body fell a little into his. Even closer to her groin, Marcus could almost feel the heat emanating from between her legs up against his face. He stayed there for a few beats, imagining what she would taste like beneath those flirty shorts. Grabbing her hips fully in his hands, he kissed each of her smooth, inner thighs, licking as he went. She uttered a moan of sheer pleasure, her hands curling in his hair as she said his name low and full of wanting.

"*Marcus...*"

"My good friends call me Marc," he said, giving her a half smile as he slowly rose in front of her.

"Are we good friends now?" she asked coyly, adjusting her clothes back into place.

"Almost. I'd like to become even better acquainted with you—if you'll let me," he answered, swiping a thumb over her full bottom lip. "You taste like lemons. I wonder what the rest of you will taste like," he whispered letting his eyes openly rove down her curvy body. When he looked back at her face, he saw her eyes were round saucers and he shook his head chuckling. Such a contradiction this one. Definitely a sexual being, probably a goddess in bed, and yet so shocked by his words. He wanted to find out more of her secrets, see if he was right about her.

He continued, "Are you sure you don't want to come back to my place? I can show you a good time, too." She eyed him, her hand coming up to finger his chin thoughtfully. He grabbed it, giving a nuzzle then a kiss. *Say yes, sexy kitten.*

"I can't." She bit her bottom lip. "Sorry, Marc, I'm here visiting my friend, remember? I promised her she could lead the way tonight, and for most of my trip out here. She's kind of my boss right now." A sweet smile came to her lips.

"Hm, I can respect your loyalty." And he was telling the truth. He admired her devotion to her friend instead of going home with a man she just met. "But I have to at least try. I would like to see you again, Simran. How about tomorrow?"

She still couldn't believe Tina had interrupted them. Thirty minutes had really gone by that quickly? As she stood fidgeting, completely caught off guard by his request, her mind raced. Was he being serious? His intense gaze gave her the answer she needed, and her own jump-started lust (not to mention soaking panties) were telling her the same thing. She wanted him to fuck her brains out. Actually, she *needed* him to. But there was something else, too, and she couldn't quite put her finger on it.

"I want to see you again, too, Marc," she answered a little shyly. "Unfortunately, my day is already booked with a whole spa and pool day planned. Um, let me see," she said, running her fingers through her hair and pushing the locks behind her ears thinking. "How about drinks after dinner? Would that work?"

"That more than works," he whispered, winking at her, a hint of the good time that awaited her evident in his gravelly voice. She laughed as excitement, relief, and mortification mushed together in her chest while they exchanged information. He stayed outside while she walked back into the club. She knew he was watching her as she left; she could practically feel his heated eyes on her backside. But she was determined not to turn and take another glance at him while the doors shut behind her.

Present Day,
New York City

Chapter 6

Simran wanted to remember back on those first few days with fondness; not to dwell on the utter mess that came later.

"Ugh!" she muttered, the washcloth leaving a wet splotch where she threw it against the TV. Her nose started to sting, and familiar tears came to her eyes. *How do I have any tears left?!* She'd cried enough to fill the Hudson River these last few months because this asshole had been so hard to get over. Lizzo's "Truth Hurts," (and really *all* of her heartbreak riddled songs, followed by those about self-love, too) played on repeat, becoming the anthem to Simran's messy life as she tried to work through her problems. She buried herself back into work and the idea of being in control of her own life again. She tried to keep it together in front of her friends; she found it nearly impossible with her sister, Sabine, though. She knew her inside and out. But for the love of Goddess Rati—the deity of love and passion she wasn't so sure she revered anymore—why should she spare more tears on Marc? The guy made his decision, had left her high and dry and she had to face it. She was trying to live by the 'thank you, next' motto because obviously they'd been on different pages about what they were doing with each other, and clearly she'd read all the signs wrong. And wasn't she an independent woman? She didn't need a man to complete her. But now, here he was, back in town and he wanted to see her. That familiar pull she always felt with him started to make its presence known, and she couldn't control her emotions knowing he was so close. She was a hot mess, no doubt about it. Oh, the fucking cliché.

His trip to Vancouver (Simran would never look at Canada the same again) took much longer than he'd anticipated. A short, two-week visit to smooth out some last-minute matters, and ensure a successful opening for his new club turned into three long months, with issue after issue cropping up. Basically, Marc's timeline got screwed and he and his business partner had to stay to wine and dine investors who threatened to pull out. After a few weeks of him being there, she and him playing phone tag, and all the other bullshit that ensued from trying to make it work long-distance (she'd done it before and hated it), he'd finally admitted that they should cool things off. Simran knew he'd been stressed out and was sympathetic to the crap he was dealing with. She had gotten busy herself with the NY summer wedding season in full swing, but his request still stunned her. She was hurt beyond words. She had feelings for him and thought he did, too. They had phenomenal chemistry, both in and out of the bedroom.

All Simran could think was what a moon-faced moron she was. What she and Marc had between them was something she let herself fall into after a long six-year gap of not opening her heart to anyone. Their chemistry was undeniable, but their conversations were extraordinary. She felt like she'd known him forever and she was so comfortable with him. There were things about herself that she could unveil, and he never laughed at her or made her feel bad for her choices—feelings that were constant with her high-strung father who she had such mixed feelings about and who was a strong presence in her life.

The thought of her father brought up that ugly break-up from when she was younger, the two inter-woven in a horrid tapestry she tried hard to forget. Her dad never let up about it, though. That failed relationship felt like a massive coronary back then, and she was convinced her heart stopped having feelings in that way. And yet, Marc walked into her life; he re-awakened emotions long buried. Then her stupid heart decided to choose him, the biggest player of them all, for the next bruising.

Mostly, she was pissed at herself. He turned out to be exactly who he always was. And Tina had warned her. Damn her, the woman could sniff out a player better than a bloodhound could sniff out a cold case. She'd cautioned her about him and his history with women. But Simran's judgement was clouded by her feelings.

Stupid feelings.

And hadn't she been the one to open communication with him recently? She'd unblocked his contact information and texted an update on the project she was helping out with. Fully not expecting a response, her phone lit up immediately after having hit 'send,' with a phone call from him. She didn't pick up, instead throwing her phone in the hamper because she didn't want to be tempted. She didn't want to talk to him after all those months. She knew it was purely about business, had to be, but she couldn't have a conversation with him. Was that childish? Yes. Was she protecting herself? Also, a hard yes. His voice message, in that stupid, sexy, gravelly voice, went like this:

"Sweetie. Simran, thank you so much for what you did. You have no idea … I couldn't have done it without you. Your talents know no limits. I want to see you, and I hope you want to see me, too. Would you meet me at The Plaza? I'll book a private dining room and we can finally catch up and I can thank you in person."

Her heart foolishly held hope, as she listened to that message hours later. Then it constricted, almost painfully. All hope squished out when she heard a woman's voice in the background, copying his every word after nastily mimicking the word "sweetie." Simran's brain easily won this one over. She wouldn't be anyone's "sweetie" again. Back to business as usual with work, family, friends, and the occasional, non-emotional hook-up (if she could be smart about it the next time around). She just had to figure out how to act around him when she finally saw him again. Her sister had a few choice words to say about the matter when she approached her about it.

∽∾∽∾∽

TWO WEEKS AGO

"Seriously, what in the honest to God *fuck*, Simran?" Sabine fumed, her eyes bulging behind her glasses. "Are you forever going to be his bitch?" she asked angrily over one of their weekly brunches at the intimate Grey Dog in the West Village. A few people at surrounding tables glanced over at Sabine's sharp tone. *Hold on to your hats, folks, the Sabine geyser is about to blow.*

Coming to Sabine for some "sisterly" advice was no easy task. Simran loved her sister fiercely, but the woman had a temper that was as unpredictable as the rain showers during India's monsoon season: happy and sunny one minute, thunder and rain the next. She needed some guidance on what to do with the fact that Marc was going to be back, and he wanted to see her. Despite Sabine's easily coaxed dark moods, she was the only one Simran really trusted about these kinds of things. Right now, though, her words stung.

"It's like, you're a glutton for punishment," her sister continued, spearing a bit of egg on her fork, and chewing fiercely. As much as Simran hated to admit it, Sabine wasn't wrong.

"Bina," Simran said calmly, trying to soothe her sister's temper before it became a full-on tirade directed at her. "I have unfinished business with him. Remember that cool gallery project he was working on, the one that offers artists from struggling communities the opportunity to showcase and sell their work? *Hello?* I've only been working on it for the past few months—" She shut her mouth abruptly at that last part. She knew it was a mistake to bring it up.

"Huh, and how's that been working out for you?" Sabine asked darkly, knowing that Simran had struggled mentally with it. Although truly enjoying the work and the mission, the constant reminder that it was Marc's vision kept her emotionally tied to him. It made it that much harder to get over his "dickhead move" as Sabine liked to call it.

"Jeez, what a tool," Sabine commented sardonically, taking a long sip of her black coffee. "He got the free labor *and* he got to ignore you the entire time. Well, you do you, Sima. Sounds like you've already made up your mind to see him. I don't know why you even bother asking me," she said flippantly. Then her face became thoughtful, and just like that, her anger simmered down. Her tone was gentle as she continued, "Will you be ok? You're going in for surgery in a few days." That sisterly warmth and concern Simran so needed from her was back now.

"I'll be ok. I just want to get this over with. I'll hand him his keys, all the paperwork, and then get the hell out of there," Simran answered firmly while she fiddled with her plate of eggs benedict. Was she trying to convince Sabine or herself?

"Mhm. If you say so. While you're at it, you might as well tell him what you and your body have been up to. Two to tango and all that shit. I'm not a fan of him, but I really believe he has the right to know," she said, waving her slim hand. "God, I'm so glad I'm over men, by the way." She was referring to her commitment to lesbianism. Simran truly wished she could say the same thing about herself.

So here she was, sitting like a fool, waiting to face the man who screwed her over. Good God would he think she wasn't attractive? *Oh, hell no, don't even go there.* This is just professional. Who gives a shit if she looked a little different? Admittedly, *she* did, that's who. She wanted to make sure her health ordeal didn't make her look weak. She needed him to see that she was ok after everything, and that she, too, had moved on, in a way. He could continue to fraternize and seduce all the women in North America for all she cared. But here was the kicker: she did care, and that's why instead of just messengering his files and keys back to him, she'd decided to meet him face to face. And here was the *real* shit kicker: she wasn't only going to discuss business, but also some very personal things that, admittedly, he did have a right to know about. She hoped he choked on the delicious sushi he ordered when she told him.

Five Months Ago,
London

9

Chapter 7

Before they met up again the next evening, Simran had to get through the long spa and pool day Tina organized. She booked massages, also reserving the rooftop pool all day for her and her twelve closest girlfriends at the Bamford Haybarn Spa. Overlooking Hyde Park, the calm retreat offered a serene oasis for the group of women.

Simran really tried to enjoy herself. Between pool time, spa services, fabulous drinks and nibbles she really had every opportunity to unwind. But she so looked forward to seeing Marcus later that every time her mind dwelled on what they would do when they met up, she felt heat pooling down to her stomach. Tina only made it worse by loudly commenting about the hickey on Simran's neck from the hot guy last night. Simran flushed and rolled her eyes. The other women peppered her with questions wanting to know more about her sexy man and she deflected as much as she could. He wasn't "her sexy man," just someone she needed to fuck her boneless. She didn't say that, just mentioned that she was meeting him again that evening and everything was super low key.

"Wait, *the* Marcus Lehigh!?" asked a cute brunette named Poppy, with oversized, bee-stung lips, reminiscent of Posh Spice from the Spice Girls. The excited squeals and bursts of chatter from everyone all of sudden turned the atmosphere into a junior high sleepover. Simran's excitement bubbled over, too, as she watched them openly exclaim over the hotness of this man. But it also sent her a big, fat, warning signal; her brain starting to work overtime in overthinking the situation. Simran tried to ignore it.

"O-M-G!" exclaimed Tina. "I knew I recognized him from somewhere." The women continued to gossip amongst themselves as Tina explained to Simran that Marcus Lehigh was the most un-eligible bachelor this side of the pond. He was loaded, successful, a brilliant businessman, and drool worthy handsome. His MO was to hop from one gorgeous woman to the next after only a few weeks. He was considered to be a god in bed, or so a few tidbits managed to mention in the rag mags. There wasn't too much about him lately because he liked to keep his affairs under wraps as much as possible. He didn't like the gossip. And when it came to people, he only let a few into his circle, tending to be a little cool to the public in general.

"And he's definitely not a settle down type of guy. But, Simran, this is perfect," Poppy squealed. "You're on vacation. Have some fun, girlfriend. I'd say you hit the jackpot. I'm SOOO jealous. I'd get on that fit beast in a heartbeat!" And all the other women tittered agreeing with her.

Tina caught her attention and said low in her ear, "Just don't get upset if he fucks and ducks, ok? Don't think too much about this. A one-night stand is ideal here, Sima. You don't need to be friends with him, he probably has enough friends, and you definitely do, too. Got it?" And she held her pinky out for Simran to link and shake. Simran returned the childhood gesture they both seemed to still take so seriously, relaxing a little.

Right, it's just vacation sex. And she continued to repeat this mantra to herself all afternoon. He'd shown a few signs of more than just the ultimate sex-god last night, but Tina and the girls were right.

By this point, anticipation completely overshadowed the warning signal in her head. Her eagerness was building, and she wanted to jump out of her skin. At one instance, she reached down between her legs to find herself wet. *Dear God.* The day had dragged on. She'd been a hermit in the sex department for about a year. Work was her full-time lover. She needed this *badly*, and it sounded like she'd chosen the best man for the job.

⁓ↄⱸↄⱸↄ

When they finally met up that evening at the Windsor Marina where his yacht was docked, she wanted to pounce him immediately. He stood there confidently leaning his back against the dock rail, one foot crossed over the other and his hands in his pockets. He looked relaxed in jeans and a navy-blue woolen pullover, but damn, he was still fine. His blond hair was tousled, and thick locks fell over his forehead into those piercing, blue eyes. Simran was still in her pool-blue bikini and maxi dress cover-up, a denim jacket hastily thrown over everything, so she was glad he was more casual tonight.

He moved quickly when he saw her approach from the black cab and pulled her into a hug. It was starting to get chilly, and his embrace was welcoming. She felt his solid chest muscles against her breasts, and it felt amazing. He smelled like mint and fresh musk again. She breathed him in and turned her face up to his, barely able to conceal her want. His ice blue eyes met her gaze and he immediately set his warm lips on hers; his tongue teasing then penetrating her mouth to find hers. He slid his hands down her back to rest on her ass and gave it a slow squeeze, making her legs go weak. She moaned in reaction. She couldn't help it. He pulled back with that wolfish smile on his face.

"Hi," he said softly.

Breathless, she said, "Hi, yourself." Oh, what he did to her. She was going to lose complete control tonight, wasn't she? Keenly aware of the ever-present wetness between her legs, a pulse started to beat down there. A rapid, yet sensually wild staccato, reminiscent of a song she'd always fantasized having sex to— Aaliyah's "Rock the Boat,"—and which only made her hornier. She had a feeling they would rock the boat to the point of capsizing it that evening. But she needed them to slow down a bit. She had some dignity, didn't she? She knew this was only about the sex, but why not milk it for what it was worth? He lived on a yacht for God's sake, and she was on vacation in some kind of fantasy world at the moment.

"I would love a tour of your boat, Marc. Will you show me?" He smiled again and took her hand in his large, warm one, his eyes still hooded and lustful as he gazed her up and down.

"Sure," he finally said, guiding her up the ramp and onto the deck.

დოდოდ

Was she playing hard to get? Marc wondered humorously. When she'd first arrived, looking incredible and serene; lush hair tumbling around her shoulders and breasts in thick waves, all he wanted to do was hoist her over his shoulder and take her to his room. That sexy hello kiss was definitely code for "fuck me now." But she was slowing the pace way down, he could tell. *That was A-Okay.* They'd play it her way. He had all night to coax out that sexy kitten. He felt the passion in that kiss and could see it in her eyes. His dick was already doing more than just twitching, having been painfully denied the night before. He'd had a raging hard-on all last night thinking about her under him in bed. But he would wait a little longer if she needed to. He mentally patted himself on the back for arranging other activities before they got busy. It was his standard operation whenever he brought women back to his boat, but he'd never really had to power through the "formalities." Something about Simran, though, made him want her on the same page as him when they finally came together. He wasn't an animal, after-all.

He led her up to the deck of his yacht, showing her around the ninety-foot space. He'd had insight to the design details, and she marveled at the glossy wood craftsmen work throughout, the two elegant states rooms below, and his master bedroom. It didn't escape him that her eyes became glazed when she ran a hand over the grey, fur comforter on his large bed, commenting on the softness. *Oh, baby, just you wait*, was the look he flashed her, and her cheeks infused with pink as she asked where he did his work. He chuckled. He liked that he could make her react like that. The library, with dark wood inlay where he staked his home office, was next door. As they were leaving, loud pop music swelled from the stairwell below. She raised her eyebrows in question.

"Come on," he said. And he took her down to the level below where the compact chef's kitchen and the cabins for his staff of four were. He led her to the kitchen where a slight, striking man with dark gelled hair boogied his body while he prepared a bountiful snack tray.

"Jon, you're going to make my guest want to hang down here instead of upstairs with me," Marc said teasingly to the man.

"Oh my God! I'm so sorry, Marc," the man said, horrified. He wiped his hands on his striped apron, turning the music down on the sound system. "I love dancing when I cook, gets me in the mood, you know," he said, turning his round puppy-dog brown eyes to Simran.

"Simran, this is Chef Jon. Jon, my guest for the evening—Simran Khan," Marc said.

"It's nice to meet you," Simran said. "And please, don't turn down the music on my account. I was, and still am, a self-professed huge N'Sync fan." And she did the familiar bye-bye hand flick from the original music video. Marcus grinned. *Who is this woman?*

"Oh my God, right? JT was so adorable with that blond-streaked mini afro," Jon giggled. Then his eyes widened. "Damn, girl, you are gorgeous. If I wasn't married to the man of my dreams already, you would turn me in a heartbeat." He looked her up and down, clutching his chest. "And Marc, here," he waved a flippant hand in his direction, "doesn't usually share his guests for the evening, so it's so great to meet you." He took Simran's hand and shook it, smiling warmly at her. But when he turned his smile to Marc, it was questioning.

Marcus ignored him. It was true, he didn't usually bring his current fling to meet his staff. There wasn't any point since they didn't stick around long enough, and he liked his privacy. He pushed the strangeness away and chuckled when he saw Simran blushing again. What was with this adorable creature? She was confident as hell; he'd witnessed it last night. But she couldn't take a compliment when it was so clearly deserved, because yeah, she was a gorgeous woman. He put his hand on her back to make her feel more comfortable and that simple touch sent a current through his arm straight to his crotch. He heard her hitch her breath, too. Christ, their attraction was out of this world. They needed to remedy that soon or he would lose it in his pants. They politely excused themselves before Jon could start on more about Justin Timberlake, and Marc smiled because he could tell Simran was enjoying herself chatting with his chef. And, honestly, she should. Jon was like a little brother to him—hilarious, kind-hearted, and talented in the kitchen. He was also a great friend and someone he personally trusted, having known him since he started his first club almost a decade ago. He didn't know why he cared about her opinion of Jon, or that they got along, but he did.

He took her above deck and quickly showed her the full bar and hot tub toward the bow. He also pointed out the bridge and cockpit where the captain and crew steered, and the swim platform. He finally led her to the sunken sitting area in the middle of the deck. She slid her sandals off while they both settled into the large orange cushions. Tucking her feet beneath her, she pushed some hair behind her ears, and he noticed the line of four diamond studs snaking up each of her earlobes. *Sexy.* He grabbed the chilling champagne and started to pour them each a glass. Jon had already delivered the beautiful snack tray with an assortment of local cheeses, caviar, crackers, pate, and berries.

"Please, help yourself. I wasn't sure if you would be hungry or not," he said. Simran thanked him and picked a ripe, red strawberry, taking a bite and moaning as the sweet flavor of ruby juices spread onto her lips. She licked the juices away, and Marc fixated on her mouth, staring at that unconscious movement. Did she know how seductive she was being? She looked up to see him watching her devilishly as he held her champagne flute out to her. Her eyes got big when they met his.

"Juicy," she commented huskily, continuing to lick the juices off, the pink of her tongue flicking out like a cat and her teeth grasping her bottom lip.

Marc grinned his one-sided grin. "God, I hope so."

Chapter 8

His voice came out in that low and gravelly tone, and again, Simran felt those shots of desire going down to her stomach and below, the heaviness settling in until they could rectify the situation. *Oh God, slow down.* She rolled her eyes and started laughing.

Taking the flute from him she took a nice mouthful of bubbly and closed her eyes, marveling on how beautiful the tart flavor paired with the sweet berry. The boat started to move away from the marina and her eyes popped open. She saw his gaze still on her, watching her.

"Where are we going?" she asked, taking another sip and closing her eyes again to relish the flavor. When she opened them again, she saw that he was drinking his champagne, but still looking at her over the rim of his glass as if fascinated.

He cleared his throat. "Well, I thought we could take a tour down the Thames. I could show you some famous sites in London. Would you like that?"

She smiled. "This isn't my first time in London."

"Sure. But have you taken a river tour down the Thames? There's nothing like seeing the views from the river." Simran appreciated the gesture, but, honestly, the views could screw themselves. She had everything she wanted to look at sitting right next to her, their bodies swaying into each other on the river's current.

"Well, I guess not. There you have it, sir, you've found out my dirtiest secret," she said impishly, wiggling her eyebrows at him.

He leaned into her, just skimming her nose with his. "Gee, I hope that's not your dirtiest secret." He didn't hold back the lust in his voice, she could hear it. *God, he smells so good.* Her stomach did a belly flop.

He set both of their glasses down and pulled her gently into his arms with her back against his chest.

"Is this ok?" he asked softly in her ear.

"Mhm," was all she could muster. She was tingling all over in a good way. He didn't kiss her, but lightly caressed her waist. Considering their scorching hot make-out session last night, and his reputation with the ladies, she'd expected him to rush right into bed, but he was being a gentleman. And she had to admit she liked meeting his chef. She'd noticed he wasn't cold with him at all, even though Jon was his employee; Marcus was quite the opposite, in fact. Was Tina mistaken about him? Did Posh Spice get the wrong memo? *Not possible.* He probably wined and dined all his female guests; this was all part of his game. The glamourous stage for his sexual pursuits was certainly made for this kind of entertaining. His yacht wasn't huge but it was both beautiful and expensive. Simran decided to settle back and enjoy, taking this for what it was: a luxurious one-night stand.

The chill was really starting to set in now as the sun went down and she was more than thankful for his warm body against hers. When the sun disappeared into the horizon, leaving blurred streaks of orange, pink, and purple, she couldn't help but think how romantic everything felt. Then Simran remembered before her heart could take a happy skip, that Marcus Lehigh was not a man of the one-woman category. *Focus, you twit, this is just vacation sex.* Because, honestly, how could it not be? She was here for only a few days and lived in NYC, and this guy was a globe-trotting player who doubled as a man-whore.

"You know Big Ben isn't really the original name of this clock tower," Marcus said huskily in her ear as the boat approached Westminster. He began to explain the true history behind the famous name, and Simran could honestly say she'd never heard someone make history sound so sensual. And then her brain screeched to a halt. *Shitballs.* Was he more than just a pretty face with a jet-setting lifestyle and an endless rotation of women? Of course he was and wasn't that how it always went—meeting someone who seemed right, but knowing all along that they were unobtainable? For Simran, smart, confident, well-rounded guys were her downfall, and it didn't hurt that he was so easy on the eyes. *No attachments, missy,* she reminded herself, yet again. He's not emotionally available and neither was she. So, to prove it to herself, she turned in his arms and shut him up with her lips. She moved them tentatively over his, caressing with small flicks of her tongue, her hands resting on the nubbly wool of his sweater. She could feel the curve of a smile on his mouth, and he started to return the kiss, flicking his tongue out to flirt with hers. He paused, hovering over her face and his tongue darted out to lick her beauty spot.

"I've been wanting to do that since I saw you last night," he whispered against her. And shivers rippled through her because that was the most erotically romantic thing anyone had ever said to her. Then he pulled her onto his lap, crushing her to him, his large hands running under her jacket up the back of her dress. She moaned at him taking control and she arched and pushed her breasts into his chest. He groaned and fisted the material of her dress, pulling her even closer to him while his tongue made its way into her mouth and tangled with hers.

She didn't know how long they kissed, lost in each other. Like last night, all time ceased to exist with this man. Finally breaking away so they could catch their breath, he leaned his forehead on hers while they took in mouthfuls of air.

"I didn't know you hated Big Ben so much," he whispered teasingly, his breathing still irregular and warm on her face.

She smiled. "I actually *love* architecture and history, but I'm not here for that kind of lesson," she said boldly, looking straight into his beautiful eyes while she toyed with the hair at the back of his neck. His brows raised in surprise and his grin was utterly devilish as his lips descended to hers this time. He continued down, trailing kisses along her neck. She closed her eyes while he started to nuzzle her, letting go to his touch.

His erection was a full hard on now. Here was the sexy kitten he'd been waiting for all night, and she hadn't held back when she pounced. Marc savored in running his nose up and down her silky skin, while his hands roamed along her soft form. That heady scent of hers: floral and earthy with a hint of spice made him feel almost high. He saw the hickey he left last night and smiled against her neck, reaching over to lick and kiss that spot. She moved her head, giving him better access as he worshipped that long neck of hers. He pushed her down onto her back and she spread her legs, her dress hiking up, as he settled his body to rest between her thighs. With his weight on his arms, his lower body and his hardness pressed against her softness, he just looked at her. Dark hair fanned around her, lush lips parted to take in breaths of air, her breasts rising and falling as the oxygen hit her lungs, and those eyes of hers were almost black with desire. He couldn't help but stare at this goddess before him. He didn't know why he was taking his time. She wanted him as badly as he wanted her, but for some reason, he sought to make their time together more than just about the one-time, all-night fuck.

He bent down, and she grabbed his head, bringing it down to hers, their lips coming together in a gnashing of teeth as he succumbed to her bossy kiss. She gently nipped his lower lip, and he groaned his pleasure. So *feisty*. Her hands curled into his hair, then ran down his back as she pulled his body closer to hers, her hips flexing up as she rubbed herself against his hard as a rock boner. They both moaned together at the delicious sensation. Marcus then moved down to the swell of her heaving breasts and kissed then nuzzled the exposed mounds, dipping his tongue into her cleavage as she gasped. He drew back and looked into her eyes, hooded now with lust, as he helped her take her jacket off. He pulled the bikini tie undone from behind her neck and she bit her bottom lip in anticipation and arched herself to him. Sliding the bodice of her dress down below her ribcage, he then peeled the cups of her bikini top off. He pushed up to look at her and he let out an animalistic growl as he took in the sight of her bare full breasts, capped with large, milk chocolate nipples, already hardened in the cool air.

"Luscious, just like I knew you would be," he said hoarsely, as he bent his head to fully pay homage to those perfect, big tits.

ↄ৴ↄ৴ↄ

His gravelly voice sent tremors through her. She bowed herself to him, wanting, no needing, his touch badly. He cupped a breast and squeezed, fingering her already pebbled nipple, while his mouth found her other breast and sipped the hard tip into his warm mouth. The pleasure coursed straight down to her pussy, and she let out little pants.

"Mm, yummy," he said against her, as he licked and teased, then sucked her nipple to an even harder point, making it shine in the dusk with wetness.

"Feels *so good*," she moaned, her eyes closed, her body bending even more toward him. He continued sucking her other breast, while she writhed underneath him and held his head to her. She felt his hand glide up her thigh, pushing her dress higher as she became breathless. *Yes, touch me there!*

"So sensual," he murmured, as his hand palmed her pussy, her bathing suit damp with her wetness. He made a sound of appreciation, and she moved her hips against his large hand. Pushing aside the material, his fingers found her slick folds and he stroked her. She shuddered as a long finger sank into her. "So juicy, just like I hoped," he crooned against her lips. She gasped at his words, not able to even kiss him back, and clenched around that finger as he slowly moved it in and out, her hips coaxed into movement by the rhythm of his hand; the pleasure building up inside her. She slipped her hands under his sweater needing to feel his warm skin, and touch his bare, hard abdomen, moving on to the small of his back. Then her hands slid down the front of his jeans to where he bulged out. She found him hard and long, and purred in delight, palming his thick length. She started caressing, moving slowly and then with more fervor, wanting to return the favor.

"Holy fuck, that feels good," he gasped, moving his own hips to her touch. "Shit, let's move this inside, babe. My crew doesn't need an unforgettable show tonight." She nodded in agreement, coming down from her lust driven high enough to cover herself and gather her things as they quickly made it to his room downstairs. *No turning back now,* she thought.

Chapter 9

When they got to his room, he grabbed a remote from his dresser and set the lights to an evening low while also turning on some chill, ambient music, which she recognized immediately. Tossing the remote over his shoulder he backed her toward the bed so that they both tumbled onto the grey fur comforter. She giggled breathlessly and started to help him remove his clothes. Before they pulled his jeans off, he leaned in to kiss her nose, asking her if they needed to worry about protection or anything else. She said she had it covered and added there was nothing else to worry about, how about him? He replied he had just been tested and came out clean but would use a condom. *Oh God, what a player, I can't believe I'm actually here*, she thought, as he reached over to the nightstand and pulled one out. She told her brain to shut up when he pulled his pants and boxer briefs off in one fell swoop, tossing them on the floor. *Hot damn!*

Her breath caught when he was fully naked. He really was masculinely beautiful. Tan skin encapsulated his hard chest, defined abs and muscularly sculpted, long legs. *Did he sunbathe buck naked?* She wondered. She would give anything to see that one day, but right now all she wanted to do was run her hands along his broad shoulders and biceps to feel the strength under her fingers. That patch of chest hair, curly and dark blond, went down to a trail (they called it happy for a reason) where his cock stood proudly to attention. It jutted up hard against his flat stomach in all its long, thick glory. Her eyes widened. It had been too long since she'd been with a guy, and judging from his size, this was her very, very lucky night. But, she had a moment of panic and her words from last night hit her—would she *actually* be able to fit him in? She looked at his face. He was watching her intently with hooded eyes, gauging her reaction, while he slowly fisted himself. Holy sacred cow, he was so arrogant and dominant in his stance. She felt her core constrict and a rush of wetness come between her legs; she was positively sopping now. She would absolutely fit him in.

"Oh, yes," she breathed as she put her hands around his engorged shaft and started to feel him up and down, her thumb flicking over his crown. He moaned in response, and she liked eliciting that noise of pleasure from him. Emboldened, she tucked her bottom lip in concentration and scooted toward him, pulling his cock between her bare breasts. She started to slide up and down as his hands came to grip her shoulders and help her move as she let him fuck her tits. She pressed her warm mounds around him, arching her back, her own moans escaping at the intimacy and the kinkiness of what they were doing.

"So erotic, baby." His eyes moved back and forth from her face to her breasts. The look he was giving her now, like she had all the power, made her lean down and put her lips to him, licking the soft, tight tip and exploring his hardness. He groaned, fully pushing himself into her mouth, and grabbing her head as she widened her mouth and relaxed her jaw to take him all the way. She sucked him, tasting his salty pre cum, her lips tightening firmly around his thickness as she went up and down his length, her hands following her movements. Going down on a guy wasn't usually her thing, nor what she wanted to start off with during a night of mindless sex, but Marc made her want to do things she wouldn't normally do, and she wanted his phenomenal cock in her mouth.

∽∾∽∾∽∾

Holy hell, her mouth was amazing. So soft, so warm, so forceful as she sucked him. But he wanted to come in her pussy, not in her mouth (yet) so he pulled away to lie down next to her. He kissed her, tasting the saltiness of himself on her lips. "Mm, kitten, that feels so good, you have no idea, but not yet. I want to pleasure you so much you won't ever forget it."

"Mm, so I can shout my satisfaction from the mountaintops?" she teased, dropping feathery kisses across his shoulders and clavicle.

"Rooftops," he corrected, reveling in her soft kisses on him, "and yes," he whispered, nuzzling her nose, "so I can get a 1000-star review from you and maybe you'll come back wanting more." Before she could process that, he started undressing her completely, tossing her clothes on to the heap with his. When she was naked in front of him, he just had to take his time to stare. She was so feminine, her waist nipped in from her large breasts, and her curvy hips flared to phenomenal legs with toned thighs and shapely calves. Her copper skin glinted under the low lights, and he wanted to bite and lick wherever her skin shone.

"So soft," she moaned, her eyes closed. The soft fur on her naked back was so smooth that she stretched and arched, seemingly tantalized in the feel of the soft pelt on the bottoms of her feet. Her natural sensuality mesmerized him as he took in the sight of her just enjoying his bed. He moved to nuzzle and suck her breasts again while she arched her back off the mattress.

"Perfect goddess with perfect tits," he hummed against her nipple, sucking hard and biting lightly, making her moan again. He trailed a hand down the soft skin of her belly to her trim, triangle of black hair. His fingers gently sought her pussy out again and found her even more wet than before. He groaned. She was more than ready for him. He looked at her face and saw her bottom lip tucked into her mouth, her dark eyes watching him. He slid one finger inside her moist heat, and she moved her hips. Damn, she was so responsive to his touch. He roved his eyes over her luscious body again and hell if he wasn't going crazy for her. He wanted to slip inside and fuck her so hard, that he thought his cock would burst. But first, he wanted to see her fall apart in his arms. He slipped two fingers inside her this time and she moved her hips sexily again. He slipped three fingers inside her, and she bucked and moaned. "You like that, kitten? Is that just right for you?" he asked softly, moving his fingers in and out of her tightness.

"Oh my god, *yes*," she moaned low in her throat. He did it again, and again, driving her toward the brink, her hips bucking up every time his fingers entered her, while her hands fisted the fur bed cover. Her moans came faster and higher pitched, breathy hiccups to his ears, and it was like a siren calling to him.

He lifted the fingers that had been inside her to his nose and inhaled. "Mm, such an intoxicating bouquet." Her eyes, hooded with desire, widened at that, and then she burst into throaty laughter. "Oh, you think that's funny, baby, do you?" He licked his fingers, smacking loudly. Then he shifted between her legs, spreading her thighs with his shoulders, and put his face up to her hot opening as she gasped. He sighed in pure pleasure at her warmth and wetness. Everything about her pussy was heaven. "Now, I'm going to taste this fine bouquet," he murmured. "Get ready, your head is about to spin," he warned, his nose nudging where her clitoris was hidden and she giggled, then moaned.

"*Please*, yes, your mouth," he heard her beg in a whisper. He grabbed her hips and gave a long, slow lick. She tasted good. Salty and sweet. She felt incredible. So hot and wet. He spread her legs wider, his tongue finding her clit and he teased, licked, and swirled it like it was the most delicious ice cream. He glanced up to see her eyes closed, her bottom lip caught in her teeth again, as she twisted and whimpered, her knees dropping to the mattress, spreading her thighs even further for him. He pulled back to tell her that she tasted phenomenally better than lemons and he could eat her out all night.

She responded by breathlessly saying, "Less talking, more eating," and pushing her pussy back into his grinning face. She was full of surprises; he'd been right about her, and he continued what he was doing. He found her clit again and he sucked hard. She cried out in pain, then moaned in pleasure as he lightly blew on the swollen bud. Dipping his tongue deep into her warmth he felt her muscles clench inside and start to shudder.

"Oh, yes that! God, your dirty tongue!" she groaned, and he chuckled against her. Nothing was hotter than a woman who appreciated the skillful use of his mouth. He maneuvered her legs over his shoulders and continued what he was doing, fucking her with his tongue, the new position giving him deeper access as his hands palmed her ass. Her body bucked and arched, and she mewled, "I'm coming!!" And her hands were fisted in her hair, her head moving side to side as she came, her body shaking in pleasure, her thighs quivering. He smiled in utter satisfaction against her new surge of wetness, murmuring how unbelievable her cunt was and he couldn't wait to slide his cock in. And, he couldn't wait any longer. He quickly came up, tore open the condom and sheathed himself. Putting his weight on his forearms, he slid his dick into her heated goodness. *Holy fucking hell!*

"Yes, sweetie, you're so hot and tight. It's so good," he rasped out as he moved further into her, feeling her muscles squeeze him inside. He gradually went in as far as he could go and stopped. The feeling was indescribable. He wanted to stay there while her soft, wet, opening hugged him tightly, letting her adjust to his size, but he wanted to pound into her hard at the same time. He had to steal himself, beads of sweat popping up on his forehead. She made him want to just do the deed of animalistic screwing and then orgasming. But he wanted to savor the moment, make her lose it again. He moved slowly in and out of her, feeling her grip him inside, and her grateful groans filled his ears. Then her smooth legs wrapped around his torso, and her hands came up his back, engulfing him to her.

"Hurry, faster," she commanded, arching her body up to his. And fuck, if she wanted faster, he would give her fucking faster. He felt her hands clutch his ass and that was all the encouragement he needed. He pushed his face into her soft neck, their bodies sticky and suctioning together, while he pumped into her hard. She moved her hips up to meet his, keeping his pace. He became more frenzied as her purrs continued in his ear, her body stayed in sync with his, and her hands gripped his ass. The pressure built up rapidly along his thighs, into his groin, and he came quicker than he thought he would. His release was forceful inside her, his satisfied groan loud as it emanated from his throat into her neck. "So *fucking* good," he rasped.

✁✃✁✃✁✃

She felt his hotness pour into her and her muscles convulsed around the force of his release as the hot shots of desire low in her belly peaked even sharper this time. *Oh, my God, am I coming again!?* She exploded, the blood in her veins thrumming. He continued to move his hardness in and out of her so she could feel the extent of her pleasure. She squealed this time, "Yes, again. *Again!*" She arched her back high into him one last time, squeezing all the goodness out of her climax. She felt like she would shatter into a million pieces or break his dick off with how good the released pressure felt.

As she came down to lay on the mattress, she continued to have small climax after-effects while they lay slick and entwined with each other; his large body half on top of hers. His hands caressed her, calming her down while the slight shudders still rippled through her; her soft moans uncontrollable. Her own words of how amazing he was incoherent to her own ears, like she was talking in some weird sex tongue.

"*Wow*, Marcus," she finally managed unsteadily, her eyes blinking back into focus.

"Marc," he corrected softly, his fingers brushing some of the hair from her sticky forehead, then he slowly pulled out to roll on to his side facing her.

"Marc, that was... God, I don't know if there are words." She looked into his face and saw that one-sided grin, along with wonderment. She knew that her own eyes must reflect that back, because that had to have been the best sex she'd ever had. She couldn't remember the last time her pleasure was put first. She didn't know what she'd done in her previous life to have the fortune of experiencing this man and his talents. His own cheeks were ruddy from their romp, sweat on his forehead, and damn, if he wasn't the hottest man she'd ever laid eyes on. "I never knew Blackmill could be so stimulating," she said playfully, referring to the sexy music he turned on a few minutes ago, her breathing still erratic. He propped up on one elbow to fully look at her face. His eyebrows shot up and his smile spread wider.

"How do you know so much about music? I get it, you're in events planning, but Blackmill isn't really mainstream, and I haven't met that many people who could knowingly spout about the underground UK club scene the way you did last night. I have to admit, I was impressed." He was gently touching her nipples and her navel, his eyes still on her own and now inquisitive. She reached up and started to finger the dimple in his chin as something akin to flutters spread across her chest making her lightheaded. Did he really understand what she was talking about last night?

"If I told you, I would have to kill you." She smiled a little mysteriously and left it at that. "What about you? How are you so into music? Is it because you're in the entertainment industry?"

"Hm, you're trying to change the subject. I'll let it go, for now, but I aim to find out whether it kills me or not," his voice was equally mysterious. Then he explained, "When I was a teenager, I used to work at a comic book-store during the summers. The owner listened to all sorts of stuff like jam bands, electronica, drum and bass, you name it. It was a really great intro to music, and I started to get interested, too. He gave me some CDs and mix tapes of all kinds of different genres...Yes, CDs and tapes," he said chuckling at the snigger she gave him. "Come on, this was twenty years ago! Anyway, the stuff really spoke to me, and I fell into a deep, psychedelic hole just exploring everything. I've learned to really appreciate it all; I feel so relaxed with music. I'm really lucky that an aspect of my business encourages me to continue expanding my musical appreciation," he finished with a shrug and his brow furrowing slightly.

Simran was amazed. Ok, so, he actually was aware of what she was talking about last night when she'd gone on about the underground London club scene. She thought maybe she'd geeked herself out a little too much because he hadn't really responded back. He was definitely turning out to have many fascinating sides and she was completely aware that if the situation were any different, she would crush on him hard. And right now, she was curious as to why he shared that personal tidbit about himself. She noticed he was a little confused himself because he looked like he'd maybe said too much to her. She nodded in agreement, deciding to just roll with it. "Well, I'm a music lover, too. I need the different genres for my different moods. It's like a soundtrack to my life and helps me get through both tough and amazing moments. You know," she continued, "something upbeat, like—"

"Justin Timberlake?" he interrupted, trying not to laugh, his fingers tracing down her hip, making her tremble.

She tried to concentrate on her answer. "Hey, I don't judge music by its cover or how mainstream it is. If I like the beats, I like the beats. And JT has some pretty rockin' rhythm. He can be a genius if you listen closely enough." She swatted his hand away. "What I was *going* to say is Queen is my go-to for upbeat, positive vibes. I'm a true classic rock girl and Mercury's vocal range is insane. Their music is the perfect companion for when I'm on a work or runner's high. Now, when I talk to my dad, give me something angsty any day, so pretty much anything by Nirvana." And she laughed at herself, looking up to see him staring intently at her, but not in lust, in something else. She went on, breaking his deep stare by looking away. "One thing's for sure, I will *never* listen to Blackmill the same way again." And she heard him chuckle, saying he was glad he could put another spin on what she thought she liked about the cool and sensual beats.

They were quiet for a bit, their heart rates finally coming to relaxed states. His fingers were still lightly skimming over her, and she was beginning to wonder if he was ready for another round. "So, purely from an event planning perspective, how did this shin dig stand up against some of your other successes? Satisfaction guaranteed and delivered?" he asked her, arching an inquiring eyebrow.

"I think you know the answer to that." She grinned coyly and then her stomach growled loudly. He chuckled softly. "Well, I'd say we *do* have a satisfied customer, we definitely worked up an appetite." He gently squeezed her nose and stood up, heading to the attached bathroom to clean up and grab them some robes.

Chapter 10

That next morning, Simran momentarily forgot where she was. She stretched within the smooth sheets and felt sunlight trying to peep through her closed eyelids. Her body felt satiated and deliciously worked, and then she groaned in remembrance. *Oh, good God, I spent the night with him.* That hadn't been in her plans at all for yesterday. Now she would have to go home to Tina and Raj's in a walk of shame. She opened her eyes and saw the beautiful morning sunlight streaming in from the bay windows in Marc's room. He wasn't there. She groaned again. *He's a morning person.*

She thought back to the night before. She'd laid sated in Marc's bed amidst the fur comforter, feeling sexy and slutty (in a good way). She couldn't have asked for more. But then her stomach growled loud and embarrassingly, and they went upstairs in matching plush navy-blue robes to nosh on the snacks and finish the champagne. He'd commented on how beautiful she was, and again, she blushed. Crap, how was he making her so self-conscious!? They'd had the best sex she'd ever had, exploring each other's naked bodies without a hint of holding back, and she had to go and act like an annoying school girl.

As for the snack tray, Chef Jon would've been pleased at the sizeable dent they made in the delicious bounty. They even started feeding each other tasty morsels, a game that started out as sensual, but turned competitive when Marcus bet her that she couldn't toss bites of food into his mouth from increasingly further distances. Simran was game for playing, if only to hear him proudly exude his baller basketball skills, and that she was no match for him. He was being an idiot, and it was kind of cute. It just made her like him more. *Damn it. I like him.* So, they literally played with their food. Points were involved, lots of laughter and guffaws, too, and it honestly felt like a really good first date, minus the animalistic, one-night stand sex part, and the fact that they were both completely naked underneath their robes. Much to Marcus' horrified (and mock) chagrin, Simran won the game (he'd obviously been letting her win by maneuvering his body to meet her tosses). Her prize? That he would have to have sex with her anywhere on his boat, her choice, which was obviously a prize for both her *and* him. Simran laughingly pointed this out but shyly and excitedly agreed to it. You know, when in Rome, and all that nonsense...

Obviously Simran had to reel in the warm feelings starting to seep into her chest again. The whole evening had been filled with unexpected twists from Marc. He was not the cold individual she'd been cautioned about, as she'd witnessed with his warm behavior toward his chef, and herself (he barely knew her, and he'd revealed some personal things). He was an absolute rock star in bed, but so attentive to her needs. And clearly, he was more than meets the eye as he shared his appreciation for architecture and design, as well as his music obsession with her; she could relate to all of those things. Simran was kind of stumped; so, pushing past that and remembering Tina's words, she intended to prove that this indeed was just about the sex. She'd climbed onto his lap straddling him, announcing that she was claiming "her" prize. She tossed her hair over her shoulder and started grinding on him while she arched her breasts into his face.

"Mm, back so soon, definitely a positive return on my investment. And you and I, my little events planner, make a pretty great team when it comes to throwing this kind of party," he teased sexily, while dragging his warm tongue through her cleavage causing her to feel a rush of dampness between her legs. This man would be her undoing. He dug something out of his robe pocket, and she saw the flash of foil under the moonlight, thus proving to her he was that player; he had freaking condoms in his robe pocket! She arched an eyebrow at him giving him a dead-pan stare. "Hey, just making sure we're prepared," he said.

"Mhm," she murmured, wrapping her arms around him, and planting an open-mouthed kiss on his lips which he hungrily returned, his tongue finding hers. He loosened her robe, pushing it off of her shoulders so her breasts spilled out in the cool air. She arched into him again, and his hands eagerly caressed and squeezed her weighty globes, making her moan in pleasure as he rolled her nipples between his warm fingers. Then his touch slid under her robe to find her lower back, right above her bare ass where, first, she giggled uncontrollably because that *was* her ticklish spot, then, repositioning his hands, he helped her grind more against him. The delicious sensation of her slick clitoris against the velvety cloth of the robe covering his dick made her entire body shudder, giving her that heavy, almost drunk feeling. She kissed his neck, pushing his robe aside to lightly bite and lick his shoulders while he told her how fucking sexy she was, how he couldn't wait for his cock to be inside her hot tight pussy again. She flushed at his dirty words, but it turned her on even more. Parting his robe further, she found him thick and long and raring to go. With her hands, she felt him up and down slowly, then picked up the pace. He moaned low and gruff against her neck, his dick getting even harder, the veins more prominent. She pushed her fingers to his base, softly exploring, feeling his balls in her palm. He tremored against her, his groan low and rumbling.

"Babe, I can't wait any longer," he rasped, and he quickly tore the condom wrapper and sheathed himself. He gripped her bare ass, lifting her up off his lap and down onto him. "Bullseye," he whispered in her ear. She was slippery and adjusted side to side to settle onto him smoothly. The feel of him filling her up completely overtook her, and her breathing became shaky, her chest constricted. She started to move on him, setting the stride, flexing her hips to take him into her deeper and deeper. And when that wasn't enough, she pushed her hips on him faster as her climax started to build.

"That's it, kitten, ride me like a stallion," he murmured playfully into her neck, sucking that vulnerable spot where her pulse was racing. Her mouth curved into a smile at his words, and she let out a long, throaty moan. God, he made her feel so free, so sexy. He reached down in front to find her clit with his thumb and started to circle her, enhancing the intensity already building up. Then he grabbed her hips and started grinding his own up into her, working her hard until she reached her peak, then letting her fall with his hands holding her. She moaned a high-pitched whimper that turned into a deep moan as she came. Anyone within a fifty-foot radius could hear her cries of how amazing he was, and that she never wanted him to stop. At that point, her body had a mind of its own. She reached down in front to rub her swollen clitoris, making her second climax trip immediately into her first. The explosions went on forever inside her as her muscles convulsed around him, trying to pull him further into her

"*Fuck me*," she heard him groan in appreciation as he watched her writhing on him, against her own hand, while coming. Her skin was glistening and her back was so arched, her head thrown back so far, that she could feel her hair swaying, the tips just brushing his thighs. She felt like a porn star as she rode her high and she was loving it. No one had ever made her feel so sensual.

"Isn't that what I'm doing?" she breathed with a grin, her body finally collapsing onto him. "God, you incredible fucker, you," she panted.

He choked out a laugh and a growl at the same time while he held her hips tightly and pushed up into her with so much force she wrapped her hands behind his neck and just held on for the ride. He stared at her breasts as they bounced roughly, and he pushed her away to watch himself move in and out of her. "You are so *fucking hot!*" he growled, and the same could be said about him as she watched his ripped abs flex with every hard thrust into her, his own chest glistening. His hands slid under her ass to bring her closer to him again and he gripped tight. "God these sweet cheeks," he shuddered, as he squeezed firmly, his fingers tracing her crack, then circling her opening. Simran gasped with shock and pleasure. She felt like he owned her body, and honest to God, she was more than fine with that. As he continued to fuck up into her, the only other noise in the cool, night air as he moved hard and fast were his deep panting and the slapping of their skin, and if those weren't the most erotic things she'd ever heard, she didn't know what was. His back stiffened and she felt it move through his torso and legs as he finally shot hotly up into her, a low, deep grunt vibrating his chest against her cheek. "Fuck, baby, it's all you. You're the incredible one," he'd rasped in gratification against her hair, his hands still gripping her ass tight. She would be deliciously bruised the next day.

Afterwards, all she recalled was them finishing the champagne, him offering her a glass of water, and then leading her down to his bedroom again. She fell asleep immediately completely spent.

Chapter 11

Marc came into his room that next morning, carrying a stack of folded clean clothes. He saw Simran stirring in his bed. Her full, black hair spread across his white sheets while she lay on her stomach. Slim arms were under the pillow her head rested on and her shoulders and her back were exposed. Her coppery skin shone in the morning light. The sight of her made him swell with satisfaction.

"Morning, sleepy-head," he murmured, as he made his way into the room. He wasn't used to having a woman in his bed all night. He was *that* guy who liked to spread out by himself and didn't need the intimacy of sleep-overs. That usually led down a path he wasn't interested in taking. In fact, his usual order of operations after a night of hedonism was to kick his bed partner out as sweetly as possible. He would then continue his evening alone, maybe prepare work for the coming week, possibly catch a documentary online with a tumbler of whiskey or listen to some music. Anything to really wind down, *by himself*. After last night's excursions, however, he could tell that Simran was pretty tipsy from the champagne and offered for her to stay over. He also didn't want the night to end. He was really enjoying her company, both physically and conversationally. She was attractive, intelligent, and funny; at times, quirky and sassy, which was a combination he didn't encounter much and found he really liked. And he couldn't forget about the sex. Both times last night had been absolutely mind-blowing, driving him crazy. Usually, he took his time with women, giving them the full Lehigh talents between the sheets. But with her, damn, he couldn't help going a little fast and wild, and the results were off the charts. He'd had hopes for a third time (hell he was used to having all-night sex benders) but as soon as he helped her down into his bed, she was out like a light. He'd stayed up a little longer, just chilling in his study then headed to bed. He'd been keenly aware of her the entire night. They didn't cuddle or anything intimate or cheesy like that, but he didn't mind having her warm, curvy body in his bed. He listened to her even breaths until sleep overtook him and strangely it didn't feel weird at all when he woke up. In fact, seeing her in the dim, early morning light made his blood pound a little faster. He'd glided his hand down her beautiful back and squeezed that gorgeous ass, but she didn't even flinch. She was still out cold, so he left her alone to take care of business and get dressed. Thoughts of persuading her for another round of sexual play this morning (if she was up for it), kept infiltrating his mind, though. He hadn't gotten enough of her it seemed.

"Just as I thought, you're a morning person," she said with a droll, as she sat up and brought the sheet up over her nakedness.

His mouth tugged into a huge grin as he took in her tousled mane and her rumpled look, knowing she was completely naked beneath the sheet. *Christ, what a woman.* So sexy in his bed, those pouty lips smiling teasingly.

"Yep," he answered. "Sorry, just my habit I guess. I'm not complaining, though, you can stay as long as you want to in *my* bed." He gave her a wicked look, wiggling his eyebrows. A blush crept up her neck to her cheeks and she tried not to look him in the eye. *Adorable.* She asked about the time and her eyes almost popped out of her head when he told her it was just about ten in the morning.

"Holy crapola, it is? I need to get a move on! My 'boss,'" she air-quoted, "has a picnic planned in Hyde Park around noon." Then she groaned and closed her eyes, her shoulders slumping.

Marc tried to hide his disappointment with a smile. "Well, sure. Is there anything you need? I'm not trying to rush you." He sat down on the bed next to her, his thigh brushing her warm one, only covered in his sheet. His body was becoming extremely aware of her nakedness now. She inhaled sharply confirming she was, too. "Simran, I had a ridiculously good time with you last night. I would love to see you again while you're in town," he continued, surprising even himself. What the hell was he doing? Sure, he was used to brief affairs, but she was leaving in less than two weeks. Even he'd been convinced when he first met her that it would be a one-night thing. But, shit, after last night, he just knew he had to see her again, had to be inside her again, just experience her for a few more days. Her eyes got big and her mouth hung open. He grinned, leaning into her. "So far only the bedroom and the deck," he ticked off on his fingers. "I need to let you win more places to have sex with me on my boat."

⌀⌀⌀

She burst into throaty giggles. "*Let* me win? Dude, I don't think so. I knew your game from the get-go. I only let you *think* you were letting me win." She tossed her hair over her shoulder and continued. "I didn't want to bruise that giant ego of yours, you know. Be prepared for a real show-down next time. How about something a little more challenging than a tossing game, like say, dancing? I'm a pretty good dancer; I've been taking classes since I was a kid and was on my high school dance team," she said smugly, her shoulders wiggling. She burst into laughter again at his incredulous look.

"I have no doubt you'd dance circles around me, given how fucking amazing your moves were last night," he said huskily, making her have to look away from him again. *Sheesh!* He was so honest, it rattled her.

"Oh Jeez," she laughed. "Thanks. It's actually been a while for me," she blurted out. *Why did I just admit that?* And now she felt herself blushing again. "I mean, I hope it was ok for you last night."

"Really? Define 'a while for me' because I'm not sure I'd buy it," he teased.

"Um, I don't know, about a year," she said mildly, still not looking at him. He didn't respond right away, so she looked up to see if was laughing at her, or disgusted, or both. His eyes were wide, his mouth open. He looked shocked.

95

He cleared his throat, composing himself. "Seriously? You could've fooled me. To answer your earlier question, it was definitely more than ok for me. You're an absolute goddess in the sack." This time *her* eyes got big at the sincerity of his words. She almost uttered out that he must be the one to bring it out in her, but was glad she held her tongue. He didn't need an even bigger head, even if she knew it was the truth.

"If you don't mind me asking, why so long?" he asked.

"Work," she automatically answered.

"That's it?" he was incredulous again.

"Um yeah. I'm still in the first five years since I started my business. It's my baby. I have to give all I can to its success." She saw him nod in understanding, but his brows creased giving her a thoughtful look.

"So, how about it then? Will I see you again while you're here? You can't deny we're good together. Better than good," he urged, his deep voice holding some of the same expectation to it that it had when they first met. What a cocky guy. But he wanted to see her again.

"Well, I mean..." She ran her hands through her hair fidgeting as she gave it some serious thought. Was she really considering this? *Take control of the situation and quit being such a wet blanket for once in your life,* she told herself. "Since our time was so ridiculously good, then I guess I *could* make time for it again," she teased, pretending to give it some more thought. Her heart bloomed while her head remained confused; of course, she would make time for him. After last night, how could she not? She'd had a "ridiculously good time" with him, too. A teeny tiny, crabby voice in her head faintly reminded her that one-night stands were only supposed to be *one* night, especially with a man who was a womanizer. But right now, he looked so damn cute sitting there in jeans and a worn-in UC Berkeley t-shirt with no shoes; such a contrast from the high-powered, well-cut club entrepreneur from two nights ago, but with the same draw and intense attraction, she couldn't refuse. She grinned because he was beaming at her, and sheesh, what a hunk, his hair tousled, just starting to dry from a shower and a night's growth of beard on his strong jaw. She didn't care if they had sex again or not, she just wanted to stare at him until the sacred cows came home. She was aware that this would be a short-term thing. She was leaving town, he was a player; *bing bang, vacation fling.* This was so un-Simran like (she'd never had a vacation fling; she always worried her feelings would get the best of her) but wasn't this what she'd been working her ass off for the past five years? So that she could enjoy life's pleasures? *Just keep your emotions in check,* she reminded herself. *Huh, easier said than done,* her brain countered.

At the moment, he was actually driving her nuts like a horny teenager with his nearness. Once again, she realized they couldn't keep their chemistry in check, and she had to get moving. But all she really wanted was to turn over and go back to sleep or turn over and let Marc have his way with her backside.

"Do you mind if I grab a shower before I go, and then we can make plans? I'm not sure where my clothes are..." She looked around for her swim suit and dress and saw them folded in his lap.

"I had the staff wash your things this morning, so you would have something clean to go home in," he said with a smile. "And by all means, please, use my shower, take your time ... there's also some extra unused toothbrushes in the medicine cabinet. Anything else?" As always, her stomach chose the perfect time to make its presence known with a loud and proud gurgle. He laughed, that low timbre of his, with his bright eyes crinkling, making her all warm and fuzzy inside. "I'm really starting to get to know your friend there," he commented.

"Yeah, it's what I refer to as my stomach monster. It has a mind of its own, really," she said, flushing.

"You need sustenance after a night of extreme sports, I get it. Chef has been keeping some coffee, eggs and toast warm, also some fruit."

"Yes, thank you, for both my clean clothes and breakfast," she said gratefully, trying to hide her embarrassment and shyness. He was so considerate; who'd have thought? He replied that it was no big deal. Then he just sat there, his blue eyes so penetrating, looking her up and down. She tried to scoot on by him, no easy feat considering she was trying to keep the sheet over her lady bits.

"Sorry," he said, standing up as she finally stood, the sheet wrapped around her. She started to inch toward the bathroom, but he grabbed her arm, pulling her back to him. "Actually, I'm not," he growled and leaned down to put his mouth on hers, capturing her in a dizzying kiss. Surprised at first, she fell under his sexy spell, opening her mouth to return the kiss as he ran his hands up and down her back, coming to rest above her ass. She giggled, then he cupped her cheeks and squeezed, and an involuntary moan escaped her. She wrapped her arms around his neck; the sheet completely forgotten and falling to the floor. He asked if he could join her, holding her naked form close to his, and she could feel his erection straining in his jeans against her belly.

"Oh God," she panted. How would she get anything done this morning? "Didn't you already shower?" she asked teasingly. He confirmed that cleaning off was not his intention in there. Yep, she was going to be late for the picnic and she didn't give a shit.

∽∾∽∾

She backed into the bathroom, tugging him with her and helped him out of his t-shirt, jeans, and boxer briefs. Naked, he went into the large shower, turning the warm water on. He turned back to her and saw her eyes taking him in, her lips parted as she stared at his already hardened cock. She walked to him slowly, swaying those curvy hips, her eyes now focused on his. He waited, water cascading down him, re-wetting his hair, droplets running in rivulets down his chest and groin. He still couldn't believe that she hadn't been with anyone in almost a year. She was a God damn sexual animal with him. He almost felt like it was his responsibility to give her what she needed after that long dry, sexless stretch. How did she not make time for sex? He remembered those crazy, early years at the start of his own business, but even he made time to have his needs met back then.

She grabbed a folded towel from the stack by the shower door, tossed it at his feet and went down on her knees. She murmured that she didn't want to bruise her knees after all and then she took his cock into her mouth, the water splashing down on both of them. He groaned in amazement and watched her. She looked up at him, then closed her eyes while she sucked his length, flicking her tongue over his rigid hardness.

"Baby, that feels so good," he hissed, his eyes watching her every movement. He put his arms out to steady himself on the tile walls while she worked her magic, teasing him, licking him, and finally sucking him with the perfect pressure and rhythm. Her hands came up to hold his base and finger him low as she lapped at him. After a few moments, his brain having stopped any coherent thought and his groans echoing off the tiles, he grabbed her head and fully pushed his length into her sweet mouth. Her luscious lips widened to accommodate him, then tightened around again and her hands came up to grip his ass. She continued to move, while husky moans escaped from her as he took control of the pace, going in and out of her mouth. God, the sensation was out of this world as she continued to move up and down his length, the sensitive tip of his cock hitting the back of her warm mouth. The pleasure intensified and he stiffened, knowing he was going to come. He grunted an exhalation of release, his eyes rolling to the back of his head, and his hot cum shot into her mouth. Shit, he didn't even have time to warn her. He continued moving in and out of her mouth as he finished, caressing the back of her head. She pulled off of him without even flinching, and came up to stand. He saw her swallow and swipe her mouth, a small, satisfied smile playing on her lips.

"What a dirty girl you are," he said wickedly in her ear. "That was fucking phenomenal. I apologize, I didn't—" She interrupted, telling him she wanted to. He planted a hard kiss on those pleasure inducing lips and grabbed his bar of soap to suds up. Then he started to clean her. She turned around, leaning her arms on the tiles as he glided his lathered hands down her amazing backside, her arms, then reaching in front to slide down her breasts, her belly, and her groin. She moaned softly, arching her back, and he knew he was going to take her for a third time soon, his cock already hardening with anticipation. He grabbed the shower head to rinse her off, and while the soapy water ran off her body, he noticed slight finger bruises on her ass cheeks. He wished he felt remorse in entirety for them, but there was some satisfaction in seeing those marks there. He leaned down low to gently kiss those bruises, murmuring he was sorry for being so rough, and he felt her shudder, heard her moan again.

All done, he shut the water off and stepped out, holding his hand out for her to take. She took it and he pulled her to him, her slick, wet body tumbling into his. He lowered them onto the plush, white bath mat while his mouth found her lips, his tongue meeting hers. He glided down her neck, taking in the scent of himself on her, to lick her already hardened nipples, then suck on them while his hands stroked her body greedily. He wanted to touch every part of her simultaneously. She panted and arched herself to him while his hand went between her legs, finding her wet and ready. "Kitten, I'm going to make this fast, so you aren't late for your party," he said gruffly as he reached up to grab a condom from one of the drawers. And, honestly, he didn't think he could do anything but fast and hard with her. She drove him a little insane. She nodded yes; her eyes closed, lost in the pleasure as he tore the package open and put it on.

"Hurry, fuck me," she breathlessly urged, spreading her smooth thighs, and raising her hips for him. He put his weight on his forearms, and plunged into her hot wetness, letting out a low growl of satisfaction as he sank in deep. He felt her tensing around him immediately, her stretching wide to fully accept him. He slid in all the way then stopped, wanting to make sure she was ok.

"What are you waiting for?" she whispered urgently, her eyes now open and glassy with pleasure. He grinned and started circling his hips then pumped into her, slow at first, then moving faster and faster, grinding into her hard. "Yes," she breathed, wrapping her legs around him, rocking her hips closer and closer. Then she bent her knees higher toward her shoulders, taking him in even deeper, her hips moving to match his own. His eyes rolled into the back of his head again. *Christ, she's incredible.* He came up on his knees and gripped her shins, holding her legs in place as he moved with speed. "*Marc, yes,*" she gasped as she clenched him tight inside her, her nails running up and down wherever she could reach—the sides of his hips and thighs. Her words were a chant in his ear as she continued moaning, "Yes, yes, yes," and he kept moving until he felt her explode inside, her cry was loud as it bounced off the walls. He felt her tremors up his length and he stiffened, letting himself go, fast and warm into her. He groaned deeply and collapsed on her, stars bursting behind his eyes as his head rested on her wet breasts.

"Damn, kitten. Just, damn."

Present Day,
New York City

Chapter 12

M arcus was a little unsure standing outside The Plaza Hotel's Hagoromo private dining room. Was Simran inside already waiting? He wondered what she was thinking, if she wanted to see him as much as he wanted to see her. He chose this particular dining room for its calming shades of pastels, and floral water-colors painted on pearl toned walls. Plus, the private waterfall and koi pond lent a meditative, relaxing touch. It was serene and exactly what Simran would appreciate.

He secretly hoped it would remind her of one of their last days together in London. They spent an amazing afternoon at the British Museum, meandering through a Japanese collection of art he wanted to show her. A few things hit him as odd when they did this, but he tried to ignore them at the time. First, it wasn't something he usually did with women in his past. With them, he really only kept things super casual and just physical. But the past few days with Simran had been something more than just casual. Their incredible multi-day, sex-bender had been sprinkled with amazing conversation, visits to hidden music stores, walks in the park, stops in bars and restaurants for drinks and small bites, followed by even more hot sex (and hell yeah, all over his boat). He'd been more than aware that he'd taken up most of her time while she was visiting her friend, but truthfully, he didn't give two shits. He wanted her to spend all of her time with him on her short trip there. When she mentioned that she hadn't made it over to the museum yet, he cleared his schedule to take her, wanting to be the one to show her around, even though she rolled her eyes and told him she'd been there about a thousand times in the past.

Second, when they got to the exhibit, he couldn't take his eyes off of her as she ooh'ed and aah'ed over the water-colored scrolls. Her dark eyes got shiny with joy over the whimsically painted pieces. She looked like the happiest kid in a candy store and a tightness started in his chest. It wasn't unpleasant, it was just strange and unfamiliar. Then, she gave him her undivided attention when he went on about his favorite topic, Samurai warriors, also pointing out an interesting display of Katana swords. She innocently asked him if he had his own sword, and if she was really good could she see and touch it later, giving him a flirty smile. He immediately got stiff in his pants. Christ, what this woman did to him, and in a museum no less.

When they reached the section representing historical Japanese sexual art, they both had to take a minute and pause because although depicted in caricature, it was still an absolute turn on. Eventually, they couldn't keep their hands off each other, with Marcus' hands finding any small reason to slide up and down her waist, and Simran "accidentally" bumping her backside frequently into his already aroused groin. They finally ducked into an alcove where Marcus pushed her up against a wall. She automatically hooked one leg around his pelvis while he crushed himself into her softness. He possessed her mouth like he was the thirstiest man alive while his hands openly roved all over her luscious body. The whole afternoon had been a turn on for him and from the way she was reacting, for her, too. A security guard discovered them grinding against each other and gave them a stern look. Before he could even start lecturing them, they ran out of the museum laughing like a bunch of high school hoodlums.

They made a mad dash back to his yacht for a quick afternoon fuck session. But they couldn't stop making out in the black taxi-cab either, and Simran couldn't stop rubbing his hardened dick during the entire ride, purring in his ear that she found his big Katana sword and she needed it stabbing her now. He was both equally amused and frenzied in his want for her and could tell the driver was more than infuriated by the way he kept muttering under his breath and giving them the stink eye in the rear-view mirror. He all but threw them out when they got to the dock; Marcus tossed a wad of pounds at him, not caring if it was double the fare amount. They stumbled onto the deck and didn't even make it to his bedroom, only to the bridge. He grabbed a condom from his wallet, fumbling to put it on as he noticed she'd already hiked her dress around her waist and her gorgeous ass was out, encased in lacey red cheeky panties. He groaned his appreciation, and cupped her ass cheeks, then pushed aside the meager fabric between her legs to finger her pussy. He shuddered at how wet she already was. She'd whined, saying they had plenty of time for that later and he didn't hesitate, he slammed his cock into her slick tightness, and grunted loudly in utter pleasure. He took her from behind, against the ship's steering wheel, a little brutally and wild. Her back arched as he wrapped her long hair around his hand and tugged, and she moaned in ecstasy. Thank God it was Sunday, and the staff had the day off.

Marc grinned at the memory, desire unfurling again in his chest. He needed to reign that in if he was going to get anywhere with her today.

He knocked on the door of the Hagoromo dining room and then opened it. She sat facing the door, on the other side of the small dining table. His breath caught because just thinking about her and scrolling through photos of her on his phone weren't enough. He forgot just how stunning she was in person. She *was*, in fact, the figure in the white shirt he saw earlier. It was her with the black hair coming to her mid back, many inches shorter than he remembered, and curlier than he remembered. A few shorter wisps in front came to rest just below her eyebrows, giving her a slight fringe. How had he never noticed how curly her hair was? Was he that full of himself? She didn't stand up when he walked in, but he could tell she was wearing a short, flowy, black dress. That white, stiff button down was over it, unbuttoned all the way and cuffed near her elbows like a jacket. She was chic, as usual, but something was different. She was softer, her face looked rounder. She didn't have her usual pop of lipstick on. In fact, her face was devoid of any makeup, from what he could tell, and yet there was a glow about her. She turned her gaze to him, smiling that saucy grin, the same as when they first saw each other at his club in London.

"Marcus," she said in that throaty voice of hers. His chest and groin tightened in reaction. He didn't bother to correct her. She had every right to treat him like a stranger.

As he approached her, her intoxicating smell was enough to set his blood racing. He couldn't believe how much he'd missed her. He wanted to hold her, touch her. It was all he could think about.

❦❦❦

She looked at his tall, muscular form up and down in jeans, a white t-shirt, and brown leather bomber. His hair was a little longer and curled a bit at the ends. The stubble along his jaw did nothing to hide that delicious little dimple in his chin and when he smiled back at her, she could almost feel the warmth emanating from him. Foxy, as usual, Mr. Lehigh, and sexy as hell. *Kill me now.* She definitely underestimated how hard this was going to be. Despite the time that had passed between them, and how much he hurt her, she wanted to throw herself into his arms. This ridiculous attraction she felt for him had to be crammed away into that part of her mind which held their memories. She mentally shook herself. She wasn't the same person from five months ago when they first met; not as carefree, firmer with herself. She could do this. *Keep it on task,* her brain reprimanded.

She watched him come to her side of the table and lean down to engulf her in a full embrace. "Simran, you look well," he said in that low gravelly voice which always made her shiver, and it was no different now. When she breathed in his familiar, masculine scent, she almost swooned. She only let him get close enough for an awkward half hug. No way was she going to let him get any nearer to her physically; that, she could control, even if her mouth started salivating like Pavlov's dog at the mere sight of him. *Step away*, she urged him silently. He went to the other side of the table, took his jacket off and sat down. She breathed a sigh of relief.

He kept himself busy by uncorking the champagne chilling in the bucket and pouring them each a glass.

Taking a long first sip, he nodded his approval. "Chef English and his staff really know their wines. This is excellent." His enthusiasm sounded a little forced, but he looked at her and waited. She didn't move immediately. His head jerked a little in confusion and she finally reached for her glass and took a small mouthful. The bubbles popped going down her throat, but she barely perceived the fresh, tart taste.

"Yes, it's lovely." she agreed absentmindedly. Then she jumped right in, not wanting to get distracted by niceties. "So, Marcus, I have your keys. The Lower East Side penthouse location is perfect, right at the heart of the cutting-edge art district, and where all the hip cultural aficionados are hanging these days. Also, it's pretty central with fairly easy access by public transportation for those artsy folks with money to burn in Brooklyn, Queens, and Jersey City. Well done. As for the renovations, I think you'll really like the way your vision came together." She was talking at warp speed and moving her hands a little too much as she spoke, but she needed to reach the finish line. "And the timeline is right on target, you have nothing to worry about there. You'll open next month, and the rooftop sculpture garden will roll out in Spring. The initial press has been insane. People are wowed by the philanthropic spin in having ten artists in residence from *only* struggling communities. And the art world is totally enthralled with the 'gallery in the sky' concept. You really do have an eye for distinction, Marcus, and a gut for what will help people. You also have a great sense for what will work," she said, eyeing him admiringly, which only made her want to smack herself. *Do you have to fall all over him again?* Although she hated him, she could still admire his professional talents, but did he have to know about it? His head and ego would only get bigger with this kind of praise. "I'm really so pleased I got the opportunity to work on this project. What an unforgettable experience," she finished, taking a huge breath of air, feeling like she just ran a marathon. "Unforgettable" was the key word. She'd known it would be an amazing opportunity for her career when she first took on managing some of the design process and fielding major press inquiries. And it had been, though first and foremost, she'd really wanted to help *him* and his mission at the time. But when things started going downhill for them, the entire endeavor ended up being fraught with emotion. A lot of the time she wanted to kick and scream at how messed up the situation became.

Reaching down to her vintage Chanel briefcase, she pulled out all of the contractor paperwork in a black file folder, everything labeled and cross labeled. The keys to the penthouse were also tucked inside. She slid everything across the table and felt both relief and emptiness well up inside her. She realized this was the conclusion to an amazing, but agonizing chapter of her life which had been riddled with *him*. Marcus reached over but instead of taking the folder, his large, warm hand captured and covered over her cool ones. She sucked in her breath and stared down at their hands, willing herself to maintain sanity. He gently brushed his thumb over her hands, back and forth. Dear God, what was he doing? He was driving her senses bonkers.

"Simran," he said gently. She didn't react. Maybe if she ignored him he would just move on with their meeting. He said her name again, the gentle roll of her name so sexy on his tongue. She wouldn't look at him. "Sims," he finally said, a little impatiently, using his nickname for her. She looked up, her head about to combust with fury, as she saw his ice blue eyes filled with kindness. How dare he call her by that loveable name. Who in the hell did he think he was?! The memory flashed back to her—the time when he started using that pet name and her heart clenched tightly.

❧❧❧

FOUR AND A HALF MONTHS AGO

While in London, she'd found a way to be with him in her short time there (secretly she knew Tina had let her off the hook because she wanted Simran to get some much-needed action). And, honestly, she wasn't sure how she could *not* see him. Their attraction was like two halves coming together that hadn't even known the other existed. It was mind-blowing to the point of being mind-bending. She attributed it to her vacation high.

Her sensible side started to creep in as her time in London came to an end. When their time was up and she had to go back to NYC, she was ok with it, she had to be. This fling would be THE best memories when she threw herself back into work and eventually got lonely, not being able to find the time for a social life or dating again. She did give Marc her business card before she left. Honestly, she didn't expect anything from him. She just asked that he look her up if he was ever in New York.

Lo and behold, almost two weeks later, a bouquet of two dozen soft, pink garden roses showed up at her door—her favorite. She couldn't believe he remembered when she'd mentioned it as they passed an adorable flower shop in the Kensington High Street district in London. The card with it read: "I'm looking you up." -M.

They caught up over the phone the next day. He wanted to see her, which made her heart secretly sing, but, realistically, she wasn't so sure about it. He was in town to finalize the financing of a new club in Vancouver. The investors had offices in Chicago and NYC, and he chose NYC because he knew someone special who lived there. Simran was touched and pleased that he would go so far to make that happen. Apparently, she'd made as strong of an impression on him as he had on her, but she had tried to close that chapter because she thought they were done. He was now breaking the rules of a fling and she wasn't sure what those rules were anymore. So, she said no, she was too busy. Quite honestly, she didn't want to have a vacation fling when she wasn't on vacation. It was too hard, and she couldn't compartmentalize it (again something that stemmed from that horrible wreck of a break-up back in her mid-twenties). He was astonished. She knew he was that man who always got what he wanted; she knew that from the beginning. But she didn't have time for these games. Somehow, though, his charming ways had broken into her fortress of solitude without him even trying.

"Come *on*, Simran," said Antoine, over drinks at their favorite wine bar. They were sitting outside, the spring air warm on their faces in the evening light. NYC in springtime, really one of its finest moments. She and her staff of three, Antoine, Shana, and Chrissy—extended family, really, because they spent so much time together at work—were taking a much-needed break after a long slog of a day. Dealing with a bridezilla of a client for an upcoming Hampton's wedding deserved some wine to wind down. "You owe this to yourself," he said confidently, referring to Marc being in town. He took a sip from his glass, pushing his round, wire framed spectacles up his nose. There was a hover of a smile under his dark, peach fuzz of a mustache.

"I do?" she asked cynically, trying to stab the fruit in her sangria. Why had she ever told these three about her vacation fling, and that Marc was in town now?

"Yes, woman! You work so hard. We all know you just got back from vacation, and you're relaxed as hell, but we also know *you*," Shana said knowingly, the beads on her braids clacking as she shook her head. "You're totally going to lose that vacation high in like, three, two, one, and…" She mimicked a bomb exploding with her voice and hands.

Now Chrissy giggled. "Sorry, Simran, you know she's right. This could be great for you. You get so anxious, and this guy sounds like *the* perfect, hmm, how shall I put it…? End of day elixir if you know what I mean." She wiggled her blond brows suggestively, her round cherub-like face smiling big. "And we're here. We can take on more work; heck, we *want* to take on more work. Sometimes you hold things a little too tightly to yourself and then you become freaky boss lady." The others nodded and made sounds of agreement.

"*Say* what now? I do not!" But Simran knew they were right. These three incredibly smart, caring, and hard-working knuckleheads were her best cheer squad, so she knew there was some truth to what they were saying. "But it could get complicated," she pushed, the thought of getting emotionally attached to a man she really did like, but who was also a self-proclaimed player, still nagged her, and she was scared to take a chance. What if she got hurt again? She didn't think she could survive it. They all shook their heads at her. "You know, with feelings? You remember feelings, right? Humans have them? They screw with your brain and make you act crazy?"

"Girl, only you act crazy, feelings or not," Shana said with a tilt of her chin. *Jeez.* These guys were really crossing the line here. Didn't they work for her? "Life is complicated, sister. We know you got hurt many moons back, and it honestly sucked balls, but that was different. This is supposed to be a little fun, right? You remember fun, don't you?" she shot back, taking a smug sip from her glass.

"That's right! Now, man-up and make this fuck buddy work for you. You need it," Antoine replied as sternly as his gentle demeanor would let him.

"Ok, *sheesh*," Simran said sarcastically, her eyes slit, trying hard not to laugh. She had to admit these three really knew her. Finally giving a defeated sigh, she consented, secretly feeling happy flutters in her stomach. "Fine. But if it gets complicated I'm coming for you," she warned, brandishing her straw at them. They nodded wide eyed and in contrition at her. "Maybe I'll invite him to your party Friday night, if that's ok, Antoine?" He was having a house-warming party at his new digs in Brooklyn. It was an over-priced "artist's loft" that he was renting with three other roommates in the DUMBO neighborhood, right outside of Manhattan.

"Yes! We have all got to meet this guy! Tomorrow night can't come soon enough!" Antoine clapped his hands in excitement.

So, she'd casually texted Marc the information Friday morning, just mentioning that if he was up for trekking out of the city, this was a quick trip over the Brooklyn Queens Expressway. It could be a fun time and a chance to catch up in person. She didn't hear from him immediately. Maybe he'd taken the hint and changed his mind about wanting to see her when she'd initially blown him off. Her heart kind of sank at that. *Oh well. No harm, no foul.*

She made her way Friday night to Antoine's place, dressed casually in a black off the shoulder long sleeved top, tucked into black ripped jeans and paired with black chunky sandals, the straps buckled around her ankles. She kept it casual with her hair, letting it loose in natural waves, and donned a little eye liner and soft red lipstick. Tossing her Chanel crossbody on, she decided to take the subway from her apartment in the West Village to Antoine's. It'd been a while since she'd taken that rail and she loved to people watch.

As soon as she stepped off the elevator at her destination forty-five minutes later, she heard a ping on her phone and saw a text from Marc. It read:

"Sorry, Simran. Had a finance meeting that lasted hours. Just saw this. Would love to join you, see you in a few."

A few? *Well, ok then,* she calmly told herself as her heart started beating faster.

At the party, her cheer squad was worse than the Spice Girls back in London. They kept their eyes laser focused on the door and whenever someone came in, they checked to see if it was Marc. It was making Simran jumpy, so she left those nerds to go find herself a drink.

She picked around the groups of guests in the airy space, crossing the expanse of floor cleared for dancing with colorful lights strobing from the disco ball hung in the rafters. One of Antoine's roommates was manning the music, spinning some cool beats, switching back and forth between the old school turntable with mixer system, and hard drive set up. She gave him a nod as she passed by and he immediately left the equipment, coming to meet her at the makeshift bar. She'd met him before and knew he had a crush on her. They started chatting about work and his life as a Software developer by day and musician (jam band keyboards) by night. She was trying to keep it casual, not wanting to encourage him but he kept talking, and she kind of tuned out because she couldn't focus.

All of sudden she felt goosebumps. When she felt a pull, only best described as an invisible forcefield, she turned to the doorway and saw him. *Oh lord have mercy.* She was in trouble. Marc looked amazing. He had the same handsome face, but if it was possible, he looked even better than she remembered. With his eyes so distinctively blue, he stared only at her, taking no notice of the other female guests who tried to move his way. Her face warmed at his look. And God, how did he make just a black t-shirt and black jeans look so sexy? She gulped as he came over to her, trying to calm her nerves.

"Hey, I'm glad I got the memo," he said softly, completely ignoring the roommate, looking her up and down in her black ensemble. His eyes lingered on her curves before coming to rest on her face.

"Me, too," she replied, her desire careening a molten hot river low into her belly. She stared back in return, her gaze taking enough of a pause on his muscular pecks, arms and groin for him to notice, before coming back to meet his face which now held a knowingly devastating grin. God, those dimples were going to make her combust on the spot. Her face grew warmer. How did he always make her so bold and embarrassed at the same time?

The throat clearing from the roommate claimed her attention back. She introduced them to each other, stumbling on the roommate's name because, honestly, she couldn't remember it with Marc standing only a few feet away. Their eyes met and they couldn't stop staring at each other, as if only two weeks apart had been years. When she heard the roommate say something about a local, underground DJ in their midst, she did a double-take. *Seriously?* Was this idiot about to out her?

"Yeah, standing right here with us. Actually..." He went over to the equipment, cutting the music and announcing loudly to the guests that THE DJ Sims had graced them with her presence tonight. Maybe they might all be gifted with some exceptional music selections from her. Everyone whooped and hollered.

Someone yelled, "DJ Sims! *Yeee-ow!*" and the few faces who knew, started to look toward her.

Marc turned wide questioning eyes on her, and she saw the pieces click in his head.

"DJ *Sims?*" he asked, his face completely captivated. "So that's your little secret, huh? I guess you'll have to kill me now," he said huskily, the pupils in his eyes starting to dilate with that tell-tale desire.

"Kill you with my music selection," she said softly, leaning further into his sexual sphere and smelling fresh mint and musk. *Yum.* "Showtime," she quipped, and went over to the equipment.

While she chose music selections, changing up the beats and fading in and out of different tracks, everyone jumped on the dance floor to grind and bust their moves. She was usually chill on the rare occasion that she deejayed for friends' parties or even random clubs in obscure parts of the five-boroughs when she had the chance, but all she could think now was, *Does he like the music I'm playing?* Marc stood on the sidelines, a drink in hand, that one-sided grin of his stuck to his face. His eyes never left her, and he nodded after each selection and rendition she mashed up, his head doing a little bop to the beats. She selected one last track, a slower paced classic that was one of her favorites, Electric Light Orchestra's "Strange Magic," before she took off the headphones and left the DJ area, leaving the song unchanged because it was awesome as is.

When she came to him, he'd already put his drink down, and was waiting with open arms. She went to him and hugged him; it felt amazing. They started swaying their bodies to the slow, dreamy music. He told her he loved this song and then he called her Sims for the first time. Her face squished up at that, not sure if she liked it or not. He chuckled and said he loved what she did up there, that she was so talented. In fact, instead of killing him, it made him feel more alive. *What a cheeseball*, she thought, and she told him so. He laughed again, the movement rumbling his broad chest, and she felt it on her cheek.

He continued to tell her he was glad she changed her mind about wanting to see him because they owed it to themselves to see where something like this could go. When she cocked her head questioningly, daring herself not to answer for fear she would ruin the moment, he honestly replied that whatever was between them was more than a fling; it was like their own strange magic that was pulling him to her and insisting she had to be feeling it, too. His tone was so sure of himself when he spoke but Simran's gaze stayed focused on his broad chest, thoughtfully fingering his pectoral muscles when she nodded her agreement, her brain having its own heart-attack. She was completely astonished at what he said, but also astonished because she knew he was right. Even if it didn't go anywhere, the intense chemistry was undeniable and how could she turn her back on that? And then he kissed her. Her cheer squad hooted in the background. She didn't care who saw them, she was lost to everyone else but him.

ᎦᎣ

Chapter 13

"**I** hate that name, you know it," Simran said petulantly, her face scrunched into a frown, as she leaned back straighter in her chair in the Hagoromo dining room. Marcus smiled, knowing she was lying and remembering the night he found out she was a DJ on the side and that she was local and elusive—something she didn't share with everybody. He also recalled coming to that party feeling like a kid on their birthday morning, excited but unsure of what to expect.

After leaving London, she'd constantly been on his mind, and he realized he wanted more of what she had to offer, even though they both agreed it was just a fling. She definitely turned out to be more than just the one-time, all-night fuck. Not only had his instincts been spot on when he felt the need to see her the entire time she was vacationing there, but he wanted her when she was gone, no one else would do. It was completely unexpected. Witnessing unstable relationships come and go through his childhood affected how he viewed his own life, beginning with how his father had left his mother when he was only a baby. After that, his mom's shitty dating record only made him feel more negative toward the whole "Soulmate/Happily Ever After" phenomenon that she was so hell bent on finding. He'd observed enough heart-break on his mom's end to last her many lifetimes and he just didn't care to take any chances when it came to long term relationships. So, he'd become a master at keeping his interludes with women brief and to the point. He didn't want, or need, the distraction making work and his career his main focus. But after Simran, he started to think there could be more to life than just the routine hook-up. Was there actually a person out there that he wanted to hold on to?

When the work opportunity came up in NYC, he jumped at the chance to explore these new-found feelings he had for her. At first, she didn't cooperate. Not only was he blindsided by her negative reaction (he was almost certain she felt the same connection he had), but the disappointment hit him harder than he thought it would. He wasn't sure how he would get through working in a city he knew she lived in without seeing her. But that surprise message to meet her in Brooklyn had him hopeful and he followed her out, eager to settle the driving distraction inside him.

He'd walked into the apartment that night and his gaze sought her out, honing in on her seemingly cool, collected stance while she casually talked to some party guest who was really trying to keep her attention. His confidence sky-rocketed in seeing her and he smirked. *Nice try, buddy, she's not into you.* Marc knew she was waiting for him. She was fidgeting slightly in distraction, twisting the ends of her hair around one of her hands. And that hair, lush and loose, was in full waves around her shoulders, cascading down her back. When she grasped it all to pull over one shoulder, exposing that beautiful neck of hers, he felt done for. Nothing existed but her. Then when she got up there, as DJ Sims, he couldn't take his eyes off of her. She was sexy as hell and had mad skills, moving back and forth eloquently between the mixer and the other equipment. Her music selection and renditions were varied and on point, moving through classic rock, eighties pop songs, into cool techno, and current dance mixes. It was interesting and clever to say the least, just like her. Afterwards, he'd made her realize that they needed to explore whatever it was between them. He'd been hesitant explaining it to her, not sure of her reaction, because quite frankly, he'd never done anything like that before. But she had nodded in agreement. He had to kiss her then, pulling her out onto the balcony to thoroughly ravish her, both of them almost losing complete control. If it had been his own place he would have absolutely fucked her out there, not giving a damn about his own party guests. What was it about her and public places? He had no restraint when it came to her. Later, he'd met her staff as she shyly introduced them. They were an entertaining crew, and he could tell they cared about her. He'd been fascinated with all of it, wanting nothing more than to be in her world, too.

Pulling his thoughts back to the Hagoromo dining room and the bungled-up present, he sighed. "I know, Sims, that's why I used it, so I could get your attention." He ruffled his hair by running a hand through it, the smile hard to keep on his face. "We need to talk. There's this ... wall between us and I want to clear the air. I know it's been a while since we saw or spoke to one another. But I hope, well, I want..." and his voice trailed off. How did he approach her about getting back together now? How could he tell her that he only wanted to be with her? He'd never done this before, and he'd already fucked it up by asking her for a break, thinking it was a good idea at the time. But he missed the hell out of her; he couldn't stop thinking about her the entire time he was in Vancouver.

Even Bruce noticed when Marc declined almost every invitation to go out on the town to "do some research." He had no interest in meeting other women.

"You go," he would say to Bruce. "Have fun, be safe, and report back your research findings." Bruce's reaction each and every time, which was plenty in their twelve weeks there, was to shake his head and comment that Marc was whipped. Or that Marc had it bad for the hot chick with the killer curves. He went as far as to say that Marc had followed *her* to NY like a dog in heat and then just dropped her when the going got too tough. That didn't end well, with the two men, normally so close, arguing loudly at the hotel bar. Marc knew there was some truth to what his friend said. At one point, he finally confided in him—Bruce having been through the committed relationship gambit before, although that hadn't ended well.

☙❧☙❧

FIVE WEEKS AGO, VANCOUVER

"It was fucking incredible; *she's* incredible, Bruce. She's like no one I've ever been with," Marc had told him a few weeks into their work trip, finally revealing what was bothering him while they sat at the bar after a long day of kissing their investors' asses.

"Yeah, she's hot. Maybe too hot for you," Bruce had joked, and got Marc to give a half-hearted smile. "Shit, now I see why you've been riding those bike trails hard every fucking morning," he said more seriously. They usually enjoyed outdoor activities together, as good friends did, joking around and being outrageously competitive. But lately, Marc wanted to be alone in the mornings during his mountain biking excursions. He hit the trails early in the nearby national park with so much pent-up energy; he returned muddy and beat-up, just as Bruce would be coming down to grab breakfast.

"But it got to be too much for me," he continued. "I've never had such intense feelings for someone else before, never had that kind of chemistry where everything just seemed to fall into place," Marc admitted to him, running his hands through his hair. "It was also taking over all my headspace. I couldn't concentrate on work. And Christ, it's still the goddamn same, actually worse that I asked for space, because she's pissed as hell at me, and won't even talk to me." He shook his head. "I want to kick my own ass for my dumbass actions with her. What I wanted and what I said to her were two completely different things. I see that now."

"So, you got scared. It happens," Bruce said knowingly, also understanding that Marc had a fear of commitment based on his parent's fucked up history. "Did you tell her that? Or did you leave her hanging?"

"What do you mean? I told her it was a good time to get some space between us since I'm up to my eyeballs here with this screwed up situation, and she's so damn crazed with all the weddings on her calendar. I thought I was doing the right thing. I didn't want to keep her waiting because I didn't know how long we'd be out here. *Fuck*, Bruce, I pretty much told her she should date other people." And he banged a fist on the bar, a tortured look twisting his face

Bruce shook his head incredulously. "*Man...*" He blew out a big whoosh of air. "So, you *did* leave her hanging about the truth, and then told her some bullshit about being with other guys. Fuck, you're an ass, a dumb one." Marc said nothing, just stared into his drink. Seeing Marc *not* react to the name calling had Bruce really concerned. He dragged his stool closer to his friend and took on a serious tone. "Sounds like you have a bad case of 'the feels.'" Marc only shrugged, shaking his head. "Man, you *do* have feelings for her don't you? *Shit*. Ok, look, here's what you're going to do: You're going to fix it with her. If you feel this shitty about it, you have to. Have you called her or tried to talk to her since?"

"Of course I have," Marc snapped. "But I keep getting her voice mail and she won't answer my texts after that last screwed up argument we had." He ran his hands through his hair in frustration. "I even asked Jon about her." Bruce raised a questioning brow. "She and him became pretty good friends when we were seeing each other. They would go shopping, or bargain hunting, or whatever it is they do at flea markets."

"And what did short stack have to say," Bruce asked affectionately. He thought of Jon as his own little brother, too.

Marc reached into his pocket and pulled out his phone, swiping around. "He literally said, and I quote, 'Marc, you're a dickhead. Fuck off about her. You screwed it up.' Even *he's* pissed at me," Marc said shaking his head. Bruce pursed his lips into his beer, trying to hide his laughter. Jon always told it like it was. Marc continued, "Apparently she hasn't returned any of his messages or calls either." He took a long sip of his drink. "Fuck, Bruce. I miss her. That voice, her feisty attitude, that incredible body." He exhaled slowly, trying to keep it together. "I plan to keep trying, like the sucker that I am, but there's so much going on here, I can't just up and leave."

"You got that right," Bruce said morosely. Then he perked up with an idea. "Look, let's get through the thickest part of this situation in the next couple of weeks; maybe it won't even take that long. Then you go back there. I'll finish up here, continue to put my charms on the stiffs." He gave Marc a hefty pat on the back. "And, you *don't* have to thank me. We all know they prefer my boyish character to your old man, reliable partner act," he joked, trying to lighten Marc's mood, while Marc pretended to bring a right hook to his gut. Then more seriously, he continued, "You have to go to her, that's your main goal. It's eating you up, man, I can see it. Tell her how you feel, and you fucked up, because, I hate to say it, brother, you did. You owe it to her and yourself. Maybe she'll take you back, maybe she won't, but at least you know you tried." And he left it at that, turning to the bartender to order them another round.

58

Chapter 14

So that was his game plan: Try to make things right with her. But what if he was too late and she was with someone else? She'd given him the cold shoulder for months, finally getting in touch about his art gallery. But even then, she'd withheld any warmth in their communication. And she was so distant right now, he couldn't read what she was thinking.

After a few minutes of silence, she spoke. "You want to what, Marcus?" she snapped, her dark-chocolate eyes going black with fury, her brow creased. *There she is.* Her full lips pinched, moving downward into a frown, and finally, she inhaled deeply, closing her eyes, then exhaling. She continued, the patience a thin thread in her voice. "You want to go back to what we had before? That's what you were about to say, wasn't it?" She opened her eyes and he saw a stranger again.

He let out a loud sigh, but knew he wasn't out of the danger zone just yet. "Well, yes, and no. Simran. Christ, I missed you so much, I can't even find the right words to tell you how much I missed you—missed us." He saw that his words hit a chord, her eyes softening. But she smiled at him as if he were a sulky child.

"How can you want something back that you tossed aside so carelessly?" She shook her head, crossing her arms, waiting expectantly for his answer. She had every right to be furious with him. They had something special, *he* was the one to tell her that when he came to NYC to find her months ago. Aside from the physical attraction and the mind-blowing sex, they laughed together, shared their interests with each other, and deep down, he cared for her as he knew she did for him. "I mean, weren't you the one who wanted to cool it?" she asked him. "Probably so you could bone every woman in Vancouver while there," she muttered under her breath, looking away, the pain evident in her voice.

He ran his hands through his hair again, one of his anxious habits. "Never, Simran. I was never with anyone while there," he told her firmly. He had left her, that was his fault, but at least this was on his side. He only wanted her the entire time.

ა৩ა৩ა৩

"Listen, Marcus, I missed you, too. I missed *us*, too. You have *no* idea." And it was all true; she *had* missed him like a missing limb (still did most of the time actually). From the moment after that party in Brooklyn, to the time he left for Vancouver, she had let him take up all her free time, time she would have normally dedicated to her business' success. He stayed on his yacht moored at the North Cove Marina on the west side, and she joined him there almost every night, maybe a handful of times back at her humble abode in the West Village, but mainly she came to him. When not working, they explored the city's hidden and most popular gems together. Eating, drinking, going to parties, concerts, and museums, and continuing to have the best sex she'd ever had, Simran's muscles were always jelly by the time they were done. It was heaven. Her sister started to miss her. And her staff happily noticed that she delegated more responsibilities to them. Everyone could agree, though, that whenever they caught up with her, they found her relaxed and happy.

Simran looked Marc over, trying to keep her emotions at bay and continued. "But I'm not an idiot. Everyone told me when I got involved with you that you were the world's biggest playboy and that I would just be one of many discarded by Marcus Lehigh. Seems they were right," she muttered.

She should have listened to Tina back then. Her best friend had been less than thrilled when she found out about them almost a month into whatever it was they were doing together in NYC.

"Just watch yourself, my friend. You're having fun now, and I'm proud of you. Honestly, someone needed to pull that work stick out of your ass and replace it with a big dick in your re-virginized muff. I can't even imagine the desolate desert he had to work with," she cackled over one of their FaceTime calls. Simran rolled her eyes and told her to shut up. "But remember what we talked about in London," she continued in a warning tone. "The guy has a reputation that you need to consider, got it? Shit," her laughter barked loud from the phone speaker, "at least I know Sabine will castrate him if something does happen." And Simran decided not to tell her that it was more than just fun for the both of them, that more was riding on the line than just "fun." And, by God, Tina knew Sabine to a T, having grown up together. When shit hit the fan,

Sabine, who had never met him, still wanted to kill him for putting her through what she'd gone through these last few weeks.

Reaching for the cool, sparkling water, Simran took a giant gulp. She could feel beads of sweat popping up in her hairline and her armpits were damp. She had to make this quick. She was physically fading and needed a big, fat nap. How quickly her hormones swung these days, from feeling great, even sexually awakened by being in Marc's presence again, to exhausted at the drop of a hat.

"Marcus," she continued, "no matter what people told me, warned me about your relationships with women, I still wanted to be with you. I really appreciated our time together, and you. I came to care for you, and I know you cared for me, too, in your own way. But then you left for work and, well, shit got too hard," she reminded him, throwing his own words back at him. The same words he used when they broke up.

"Wait a minute, Simran," he interrupted with a hand up, "I was being honest with you. You're going to punish me for honesty? Isn't that the 'golden rule' for any God damn relationship? And I tried to contact you, but you never returned my calls," he pointed out, his sharp jaw clenched, looking like it could cut ice, and the light blue of his eyes so murky and stormy with emotion.

She flushed. He had a point, but she was irritated as hell that he was dishing out relationship dos and don'ts right now.

"Don't go throwing relationship advice my way, Marcus. You're the last person who should be doing that," she said hotly. Fuck, she needed to cool it before she really blew a gasket at him. She took a deep calming breath. "And, yes, I know I never returned your calls. I got really busy with … some personal things." Why did she feel so bad? He was the one who broke it off with her. She never agreed to stay in touch, even though he wanted to.

It sounds like there's someone else, he thought darkly. What did he expect? He hadn't held her to any commitment. Sure, it would have been nice to catch up over the phone, even if they weren't involved anymore. It would have been great to hear how she was doing. But she didn't want to talk to him, that was evident by the silence from her end. What was he doing here? Was this a lost cause between them? He felt a punch to his gut because he was the one who pushed her away.

"Simran, I didn't anticipate so many problems cropping up at our club opening, you know that. I didn't want to string you along because I didn't know how long I would be gone. You deserved better than that. But I'm here now, and I want to see if we can pick up where we left off, maybe move things further in our relationship than it was before," he finished. He had so much hope in his chest and felt so bare laying out his need for her, to her. The silence was deafening, but he waited. If she confirmed that there was someone else in her life, he knew he would be crushed. She was like no other person he'd ever been with, and he couldn't get enough of her, but he realized it too late, it seemed.

"You want a relationship again, *now*?" Her dark eyes were wide with astonishment. "You think I'm going down that rabbit hole, after *everything* that happened?" Now he was confused but she continued, shaking her head, "Come on, Marcus. Once a player, always a player. I don't think you're capable of a relationship that lasts for more than, what was it with us, about three months? That's a new record for you, and a lofty goal to uphold." He frowned, the words burned deep, searing his chest.

"Simran, I may have been a player in the past, but my relationships were all consensual, you know that," he defended himself. How many times had they gone over this? "Not one woman I was with ever held it against me that our time together was too short. When our time ended, we both agreed and went off on our own ways." Didn't she realize that he wasn't the bad guy here? He crossed his arms in front of his chest, feeling like he was being cross examined. Why were they discussing his past? He wanted to discuss their future, but she wasn't having any of that.

She snorted loudly. "Seriously?! How do you know? God, you're so conceited, Marcus. Maybe they did hold it against you, just not to your *face*," she said with a hint of disdain, her eyes slit. And he wondered how the hell they had gotten to this point. She really wanted to hurt him, didn't she? They were like two strangers arguing. All he wanted to do was go to her, hold her, and never let her go. He didn't want to be on the receiving end of her anger and disgust.

He huffed out his own anger. Nothing was ever easy with this woman, and he was a fucking fool who was still chasing after her. "Listen, Simran, if there's someone else, just tell me. I'm a big boy, I can handle it." He was lying. Could he handle it? Fuck no. He would need to sell his yacht and anything else that held memories of her, of them, and disappear for a while.

⁂

"Regardless if there's someone else, or not, do you think I would be dumb enough to try with you again?" she scoffed. Seriously, the arrogance dripping off this man was going to kill her if she didn't strangle him first. Did he really think she would just fall back into his arms, and they would go on their merry way? He was a moron when it came to relationships and emotions. Then she noticed his forehead wrinkled, his mouth agape and she could tell her words had hit him hard. She realized it didn't feel as great as she thought it would; her own self-assured high at kicking him when he was down was starting to crumble.

Taking a deep breath, she dug into the truth. "Ok," she said a little nervously, licking her lips. "Ok. Look, there was someone else." And she saw how wounded his eyes became; how his handsome face contorted into agony. Oh shit, she needed to be strong and get through this, not feel sympathy toward him. "I was *pregnant*, Marcus. I was pregnant with *our* child," she confessed. *You asshat*, she finished silently. He was stunned now, his eyebrows so high on his forehead, they almost reached his hairline. She went on, "I found out a few weeks after you left which was when things started to go downhill for us. I was going to tell you, but I made the decision not to after that shitty last conversation we had." His gasp was loud in the intimate dining room and his face was mottling red with anger. "I know, I know," she conceded with a hand up. "You had a right to know, but it is what it is." She shrugged. At the time, she just didn't want him to know because she was so hurt by him. On reflection, she realized it was extremely childish and spiteful. "Anyway, it surprised the hell out of me because, you know, I was on birth control. Did you know there's about a nine percent chance you can still get pregnant, even *while* on the pill? I mean, I knew the odds," she rambled, talking with her hands again, looking everywhere but at him, "very small odds, but somehow one of those little suckers found a way. I mean, we used condoms, but there were those few times we just didn't, remember?" Her face grew warm at those erotic encounters. When putting on protection, even just those few seconds, seemed to take *too* much time, because their passion was so all consuming that they just needed to be connected physically

She paused to catch her breath. She knew she sounded crazy, but she didn't care, she needed to tell him. "Anyway, you and I, that wasn't happening, so I thought, screw it. I'm a grown-ass woman. At thirty-two years old, I should be able to do this. And you know what, I was actually relieved with my decision. I was honest to freaking God happy to have a piece of you growing inside me. And that's when I realized I had fallen for you. I already cared about you before, but knowing I wanted to keep the baby on my own, made me realize *how much* I cared for you. I know, this is all shocking. I mean, imagine how I felt seeing those little pink lines!" He was leaning back in his chair still dumbfounded, no words forming on his lips, so she went on. "Things were going well. I was at my twelve-week ultrasound when … they found no heartbeat." She stopped, remembering how alone she felt in that room with just the nurse technician telling her how sorry she was that the pregnancy wasn't viable. It happened so quickly that Simran thought there must have been a mistake. She asked her to check again. The nurse only shook her head sympathetically and said there was no mistake. But she checked again for her anyway, and in doing so found something else.

"So … no heartbeat," Simran continued, swallowing hard, driving down the pressure rising into her throat, "but on the upside, if you can even call it that, they found something else. There was an abnormally enlarged cyst on one of my … ovaries." How detailed should she go? She decided to just push through, no turning back now. "It was there before but had grown. I mean, it was huge, like over three inches huge," she showed him an approximate size, spacing out her index finger and thumb. "And because of my family's cancer history, they had to remove it immediately and run some tests. Also, there was a huge chance the damn thing could burst inside me. I could end up in the ER with worse consequences. So, all of that," and she waved her hand in a circle in front of her face, "combined with the fact that the … fetus, um, wasn't coming out on its own…" Now her face was hot with embarrassment. *Please Goddess Durga, eliminate my suffering and make the floor swallow me up whole right now.* "Well, I had to go in to have both, um, removed, one right after the other. Actually, I just went through both procedures a few days ago, one right after the other; like killing two birds, you know? I'm still recovering and have all these crazy pregnancy hormones in me. I mean, look at my *hair*, it's never been so curly! I don't even know what to do with it!" She laughed lightly, trying to regain some semblance of her old confident self as she ran her hands through her loose curls. "And I'm exhausted all the freaking time. It really blows, the side effects of pregnancy, with no baby to show for it." *Oh crap, wind it down, Simran.* "I won't know for a few days if the cyst is cancerous or not." All the words finally tumbled out of her and then she stopped abruptly, looking down at the table. She had to catch her breath and take another long gulp of water, finishing the glass.

Was he disgusted right now? No way could this level of reality ever fit into his sexy and luxurious, cushy lifestyle. *Fantastic.* This would make it so much easier to say goodbye for good. She could start afresh with herself in a few weeks, or a few months ... or whenever she felt better. She checked the clock on her phone. Only one more hour until pain meds, thank the good freaking lord!

Chapter 15

Marcus' ears filled with a loud buzzing that only increased as she told him her ordeal. This had only ever happened to him one other time in his life, when someone else he cared for was hurt by his actions. He snapped out of it when she stopped talking.

"*Holy shit*, Simran," he said, his voice low and raw, filled with varying emotions. Shocked didn't even come close to what he was experiencing. He didn't know how to respond, something that didn't happen very often with him. He let out a huge huff of breath; his hands in his hair again. He couldn't believe what he had put this incredible person through. Of course, he hadn't heard from her. She was dealing with so much. This mess was both of their faults, and he'd abandoned her. Not to mention possibly *cancer*?! And here he was, an arrogant prick asking if they could go back to what they had a few months ago. But that wasn't entirely true. He wanted so much more, but could he really ask that of her now? He raked his hand through his hair again, completely mussing any semblance of it, thick locks falling into his eyes. He felt the fury trickling in, too, his head starting to pound from it. She was pregnant and hadn't told him.

She stood up suddenly and he followed, getting to his feet, too, because they were far from done talking. Her napkin fell from her lap, and she stood wobbling in her black heeled booties, her hands gripping the chair. He instinctively came closer to steady her, and he noticed how flushed she had become, moisture beading her forehead and upper lip. He could smell her familiar scent, but it was mostly masked by the dank smell of sweat.

"Marcus, I'm sorry, I have to go now. I don't feel well."

He grabbed her around the waist and felt her clothes soaked with moisture. All worry for her took over anything else he was feeling. "What can I do, baby? How can I help? Where's your room?" She didn't say anything just reached for her briefcase, dug around inside, then handed him her key card. She was in a suite on the floor below him. He took her bag, the files on the table, and had her lean on him as they went to the door. A server was just coming in with a fresh platter of delectable sushi and sashimi. Marcus told him that dinner was over and instructed him to charge his account and thank the Chef personally for him. Then he gently led Simran to the elevator banks where they whisked up to the nineteenth floor.

He opened her door and lightly pushed her inside. After putting everything down, he helped remove her soaked white shirt. Crouching down in front of her to take her boots off, a brief memory hit him hard. The memory of another time he'd been in this same position when they first met, so different in experience than today. Moving his hands to the hem of her dress, he started to lift it in order to get her out of the damp material, and she furiously pushed his hands away.

"*Don't*," she groaned in annoyance and pain. She stumbled slowly to the other side of the room where the bed was and sat down on one side. Without pulling the covers back (which he knew was a hotel room pet-peeve of hers; a ridiculous argument they'd had over his decision to stay long-term in a Vancouver hotel), she lay down. Glancing around the room, he could tell she'd been there for a while, perhaps staying to recoup after her surgery. She would have anything she needed just a phone call away, and her sister was nearby in a hotel apartment, a perk as Head of Guest Affairs.

He went to the bathroom and saw the different pain medication bottles on the counter. After filling a glass with cold water, he brought it and the bottles to her.

"Simran, which one?" he asked.

"The blue bottle, but it's not time yet. I have about an hour before I can take another one."

"Ok. What can I do for you right now, baby?" he asked, his concern for her overwhelming him again, but he wanted to stay and help.

"You can go." Her voice was flat as she buried her face in the pillow and curled into a ball. She looked so vulnerable and small in that bed, and his chest constricted. Marc did the only thing he knew would make either of them feel better. He took off his jacket and sat down, the mattress dipping. She looked up baffled and then rolled herself away, turning her back to him. He lay down and scooted next to her, putting a hand on her waist. The touch sparked that familiar fission between the both of them and Marc closed his eyes at the completeness of that feeling. She didn't move away, so he dared to wrap an arm around her waist. Then, he couldn't help it because he was curious, and knew she was hurting, so he started to caress her belly, feeling the space where a life had grown for the briefest of moments. She sucked in air sharply, and he removed his hand immediately. He sighed again, this time in frustration, and moved away from her onto his back.

"Why aren't you listening to me, why are you still here?" He heard her ask sluggishly, then, silence. He leaned over to see her eyes closed and her breathing even. She was asleep, her face resting peacefully for the first time since he had seen her again.

He lay on his back, one arm under his head as he replayed their previous conversation. God, he was such a jackass. How many reasons had he already given her to *not* be with him again? Too many to count, that was for sure. And she hated him, he could feel it radiating from her. But she had seen him. That was something, wasn't it? She admitted she cared for him, had fallen for him back then, and that was his shining beacon. He could work with that, whatever it took.

She turned onto her back, and groaned, her eyes half open and glassy. She mumbled something incoherently, her head moving back and forth on the pillow, making her hair a black cloud framing her face. She was in some deep dream state but was shifting around trying to get comfortable. She needed her rest. Marc put a hand on her waist, and she didn't flinch. He tried to comfort her again by scooting up next to her, careful to keep some space between their bodies. He gently pushed a hand through her hair, sliding his fingers along the smooth strands to her scalp. He knew she was a sucker for head massages. She had said she found them better than sex; well, at least before she had met him and his ecstasy driven highs, she'd admitted. For her, a good head massage was the key to her heart. She had embarrassingly leaked that to him back in London when they'd been splayed in the sitting area on his yacht, and he couldn't keep his hands out of her long, silky locks. He smiled at that memory, rubbing her scalp in the soothing way she liked. She moaned and purred in her sleep, making him have to push his desire to embrace her way, way down. She finally fell back into a deep slumber, one that wasn't mottled with bad dreams he hoped. He removed his hand and just watched her sleep.

❧❧❧

She awoke to him sitting in one of the plush chairs facing the window.

"What time is it?" she asked groggily, slowly sitting up, a blanket she didn't remember covering herself with fell around her waist. It was dark outside. How long had she been asleep? Had he been here the whole time? Marcus came to sit next to her on the bed.

"Hey," he said gently, a small smile on his lips. The strap of her dress had fallen down, and he pulled it back up, then reached to smooth her hair. She unconsciously leaned into his touch, closing her eyes. "You've been out for two hours. I didn't want to wake you. Do you want to take your meds now?"

"Yeah, thanks," she said softly, still shocked he was there. Had she dreamt it or was he the one who had massaged her back to sleep? He knew she absolutely adored that, and it was so soothing she fell into a deep, dreamless slumber like she was drugged.

He handed her the pills and water and she gulped them down, drinking the water thirstily. She wiped her mouth with the back of her hand as she looked up at him. He didn't have to be here. Couldn't he just leave? She had this under control, she was fine. And as she told him so, her stomach betrayed her, giving a loud gurgle of hunger. Marcus smiled at this all too familiar friend of theirs: Simran's hungry stomach monster.

"Do you have food to eat? We missed dinner. I can't imagine it's good for recovery without some protein and a solid meal." Simran rolled her eyes at this know-it-all, but she knew he was right.

"I didn't order dinner because I *thought* we would be eating earlier," she said. He swiftly moved to the phone and began ordering room service: the best steak dinner on the menu with sides of creamed spinach and baked potato, for two. What the hell did he think he was doing? God, he really was so full of himself.

Sighing, too tired to argue, she conceded, "Listen, if you're going to stick around here for a bit, I need to get something in my stomach asap." They both knew she would get hangry (an angered hungry person) if she didn't eat when she was hungry. "There are protein bars in the fridge. Could you grab me one?"

He did so wordlessly, opening it and handing it to her. She took a few bites and chewed thoughtfully. Then she stood up slowly. "I need to rinse off." He nodded and gently guided her to the bathroom. While she searched her belongings for a hairband to pull her hair back, he turned the shower on to let the bathroom steam up.

"Do you need help with undressing?" he asked, their eyes meeting in the mirror. She saw his bright ones darken, holding that familiar hunger, and her traitorous body reacted with that deep desire unfurling from her chest into her stomach. *Nope.*

"I think you've helped enough for now." She turned her back to him while she pulled her hair up into a bun. He retreated, leaving the bathroom door half open in case she needed anything.

She looked at herself in the mirror, disgusted. She felt gross and crusty from the dried sweat. So much for not looking weak in front of Marc. She slowly pulled the straps of her dress down, slipping it off over her legs and kicking it into a corner. She winced at her reflection. Her abdomen usually had a slight curve to it which she came to love, but now, there was a slight pooch. To make matters worse, she had three spots covered in bandages on her lower stomach where the doctor made incisions to remove the cyst. She knew she would have scars leftover. She knew it wasn't Marc's fault, but goddamn it how she wanted to blame his stupid face for this.

She pushed her boy shorts down and stepped into the steamy shower, hoping the water would relax her and rinse off the welling anger and sadness in her. She was such an idiot for seeing him again. And yet, she had a glimmer of positivity in her. He'd been as miserable as she had been in their entire time apart. It wasn't satisfaction she had rising inside her knowing that he'd been a sad sack (well some of it was), but she was relieved that he hadn't ended up being the cold-hearted man she was beginning to think he was after they broke up. She hadn't wasted her feelings on an asshole. At least she could leave this relationship without feeling like she'd been the biggest fool.

⚜⚜⚜

While she showered, he waited for room service. He pulled up a work article on his phone, but the words were written in Mandarin for all he knew because his concentration was shot. He didn't mean to watch her as she undressed, he just wanted to make sure she was ok. He could see her reflection in the mirror and her body was just as luscious as he remembered, making him want to grab her and kiss those pouty lips. Her stomach was protruding out a bit, the space created to carry their baby, and he caught the site of white bandages on her stomach. But Christ, she was still such a sight to behold naked that he had to turn away.

His thoughts shifted to the lost baby. If it had lived, would Simran have told him, even if he never came back to fix things with her? Or would the child be kept a secret, growing up in the bosom of her family and friends here on the east coast and parts of India? What if their child would want to know *him*? His heart missed a beat at the thought. Admittedly, this more than bothered him. The worry for Simran was replaced with his forgotten anger about being in the dark about her pregnancy. He was a thirty-seven-year-old man who never had an interest in kids. He himself didn't have a father figure growing up, something that he and Simran had talked about before. But, damn, the idea of having a child with Simran didn't turn him off. Actually, he felt quite the opposite and that astounded the hell out of him.

His thoughts were interrupted by a swift knock at the door and the call of room service. After the food had been wheeled in and set up in the dining area, Marc set out cutting up the wagyu T-bone into proper parts, needing something to keep himself busy. Simran needed sustenance to get healthy again and that he could happily help her with.

His mind wandered back to when they opened up about their parents and touched on parenthood. It had also been an eye-opening moment giving him a glimpse into the other world Simran dealt with, her Indian side.

It had been a few weeks since he'd been in NYC and Simran had been MIA for a few days, attending an Indian wedding in the city. She explained that it was a huge, colorful, and celebratory week-long affair. Ceremonies, socializing, dance, food, and drink filled up her time, which meant she wasn't available except for some extremely dirty, late night phone sex with him. Both of them were breathless when they hung up, and not as fulfilled as they hoped they would be. He could tell she was worn out by the end of each night, so he didn't want to bother her by dropping in at her place and making her even more exhausted with sex. By the last day's final event, though, she'd had enough celebrating and snuck away from the party to come see him.

Chapter 16

FOUR MONTHS AGO

She arrived in the early evening at his yacht. He was waiting for her, and when she stepped out of the taxi, his jaw dropped. The pictures she sent of herself during the events' highlights wearing different traditional clothes were beyond cool. She looked stunning in everything, and the colors were vibrant and festive. But seeing her in person in all her glory made his pulse beat faster and pure lust run straight through him. His cock stirred to attention quickly, an effect only she had on him he realized.

Her sheer, black sari swathed around her lower body, like a present ready to be unwrapped, and the hem was trimmed with sparkling gold. The gauzy material skimmed low on her waist, along the soft skin of her stomach below her belly button. The front part (the *pallu* he later learned it was called) was artfully slung from the front to the back, covering her chest in a filmy layer of black. It did little to conceal the tight, gold cropped top blouse she wore underneath, her full breasts straining against the material. The back of the *pallu* trailed behind her, in an expanse of more sparkling gold detail—

fireworks glittering in the wake of a goddess like Simran herself.

She stood barefoot, having taken off her heels and holding them in one hand, as the driver pulled out her overnight bag. She thanked him with a smile and came over to Marcus. Up close he could see the heavy, black liner drawn around her eyes, rosy cheeks, and barely-there, red lipstick. She had a black dot on her forehead and wore lots of heavy, gold jewelry. Her hair was down in black waves which blew in the wind as they met up. He let out a long and slow, wolf whistle. He couldn't help it.

"You are absolutely exotic," he crooned, reaching for her. Her hands came up to keep the hair from blowing into her face and he saw the intricate henna detail painted on the backs of them. The delicate glass bangles that lined high on her arms tinkled with her movements.

"Oh, *Jeez.* Marcus Lehigh, that is so cliché," she said a little harshly. She was tired, he could tell, but he hadn't expected this. He stopped up short from giving her a kiss.

"*What?* What did I say? I mean..." He pushed her back to his arm's length so he could take a good look at her again, his eyes lingering on every curve she offered. "You are to me," he said as gently as he could, and her face relaxed. His work in Asia had exposed him to some aspects of South Asian culture, but he would never consider himself an expert. So, he was curious as to why she thought the way she did about his compliment.

Simran reigned in her annoyance. It wasn't fair to Marc. For her, life was complicated as a first-generation Indian woman living in a western country. She was well acquainted with racism and the microaggressions sprinkled throughout the everyday lives of first- and second-generation South Asians. She'd experienced much of them first-hand since her move from India to the US as a little girl. On top of that, being a woman in a very masculine arena like the South Asian culture was aggravating. She was just so tired from all the hoopla of the past week. Guests, from close relatives to acquaintances, interrogated her about why she wasn't married yet, not giving a flying fuck about her career successes. Straddling two strong cultures was mentally exhausting. She didn't expect Marc to know all this. All she wanted to do was fall into his strong arms and let him have his way with her. But she decided to try to start somewhere with him. This issue was a huge part of her life that he needed to understand, or they could never work out.

"Babe, it's just that ... *that* is a pick-up line I've heard all my life from one random non-Indian dude or another. It's, I don't know, kind of demeaning and a little gross. What I have to offer is me, who I am ... my personality, interests, my successes or non-successes as a person. Yes, I'm a self-respecting brown woman who is proud of my Indian culture ... well not some parts, but I don't see my culture as something that should define why you're attracted to me. Don't only admire those attributes you find so different, or even *exotic*."

She huffed some air out, blowing off hair that was sticking to her face. Frustrated because she didn't think she was doing this topic justice, she continued, "It's complicated and hard to explain. God, I'm probably really botching it up right now. I mean, ok, I don't fall at your feet because of your whiteness, or mixed European back-ground." Now she was flustered and felt like an idiot. "And listen, I won't play any silly belly dancing games with you. Especially since that isn't even the right culture," she finished, crossing her arms to protect herself from what was surely going to be humor in his reaction.

He grabbed her chin so that he could look straight into her eyes. "I apologize, Simran. I didn't mean to offend you." His voice was soft and his own bright eyes sincere. "But you excite me. You're different from any woman I've been with, and you know what, in that you *are* exotic. Forget about your Indian culture. You're beautiful, sexy, funny, smart, sexy ... I know, I said that twice," he said grinning. "I can't help the way I feel. I'll try to re-phrase next time, so I don't offend you. I love that I can learn from you. And, since we're talking about it, I'm actually a quarter German, fifty percent Scandinavian, and a big mash up of Europeanism the rest of the way. I think the widely used, but somewhat offensive term is 'mutt'? But, hey, I can tell you all about bratwursts and fjords if you're ever interested," he finished, humor only now filling his gorgeous smile.

She fingered that dimple in his chin while she thought about what he just said. His honesty caught her off guard and she realized that of course there were other forms of microaggressions in the world that had nothing to do with skin color or Asian culture. He had a point, but she was relieved he was trying to understand where she was coming from. It was no doubt the closest thing to a statement of caring that she would probably ever get from a man like him. So, she pushed herself into his arms and snuggled deeply into his broad chest.

"You're forgiven," she sighed. "And I would love to hear more about bratwursts and fjords. But, you know what they say about brats. They're the wurst. Get it, the wurst?" she asked snorting at her own terrible joke. "I'm sorry, that was awful. I'll do better once I've had your sausage in me," she continued, her shoulders quaking as she couldn't control her tired giggles.

He chuckled, stroking her hair. "Baby, quit while you're ahead." His breath was warm against her ear. "Goofball," she heard him mutter under his breath, and his arms tightened around her. Then he stunned her by what came out of his mouth next. "Damn, Simran, you're the most beautiful American woman wearing Indian traditional clothes I've ever seen." She sucked in her breath, looking up at him. His eyes were earnest, and he had such a warm smile on his handsome face. "See, I'm trying," he said wolfishly. And she had to admit, he was. She reached up and planted a passionate kiss on his mouth, leaving them both breathless. He grabbed her bag and they headed onto his boat, into his room.

When she started to take off the heavy, gold jewelry, he stopped her. "No, baby, can you leave it on?" She had to pause for a minute to think about it. She was actually torn because she wasn't sure if this was icky white man behavior, or just sexy play to spice things up. She decided on the latter. It was a turn on for her, too. The glass bangles had to come off, though, because those would *definitely* be hazardous in sexual play. She started to unpin the *pallu* at her shoulder and gave a big sigh of relief. Removing her sari was always so freeing. She loved wearing traditional clothes and getting fancy for special events, but a few hours in she always felt a little confined, trussed up like a glammed-up present. As she started to unwind the yards of fabric, Marc stopped her again as he turned on some music. Blackmill's melodic music, with the sensual—almost erotic—beats washed over them. "Undress for me, kitten." He laid on his back on the bed in just his black boxer briefs. Holy Durga, mother of the universe, what a hunk. He was so comfortable with his long legs splayed out, one muscular arm bent behind his head and his other hand disappearing into his briefs. His ab muscles flexed on the upward strokes he gave to himself. He looked like a cross between a male model and an exotic dancer, but with chest hair and that oh-so-happy trail which made him so manly. His pheromones were talking to hers on another level right now and she was feeling that trippy sensation she always felt when she was aroused around him. How did she get so lucky with this stud of man? And he wanted her.

His cock was starting to tent up his underwear and now she couldn't deny that her body was more than tingling in anticipation. She lifted an eyebrow at him as if to say, *oh, yes, I see where you're going with this, Mr. Lehigh.* Facing him, she let the sheer black material of her *pallu* fall to the floor in front of her. Then she unwound the rest of her sari, letting it all drop in a shimmering black and gold puddle at her feet. She stepped out in just her black petticoat and gold blouse, her hands on her hips.

Marc's eyes roved heatedly over her, stopping at her breasts. How could he not? She knew they were pushing against the tight fabric of her blouse. The snug look was so in fashion now and did nothing to hide the fact that her nipples were already hard. He watched as her hands slid up her waist to fondle her own breasts, pinching the tips. She moaned at her own actions and Marc nodded his head, growling a low "yes," as he rubbed himself, his eyes on her. She swayed her hips, rolling her torso, and continued to run her hands up and down her body and over her breasts. What was it she said about not doing any belly dancing? Her hips had a mind of their own, wriggling to the pulse beating in the room that mirrored the one between her legs.

As she started to untie the ribbon holding her petticoat on, he moved to her and gently pushed her back up against the wall, taking over. "Impatient much?" she teased, while he knelt before her, sliding both the material and her black, lace panties off together. She heard him growl another "yes" and "I'm hungry," while he lifted one of her smooth legs over his shoulder, pushing his face into her. She moaned in anticipation, her fingers sliding through his thick hair.

"Fuck, kitten, so hot and wet for me already," he murmured against her sensitive mound, and she trembled, whimpering at the touch of his tongue. He licked and explored, continuing to tell her how good she tasted, how he couldn't get enough of her sweet pussy, while she panted. This was what she had been waiting for all week.

He found her clit and sucked gently until it was swollen. Then he sucked hard, just the way she liked it and she cried out while his mouth worked her. She pushed herself further into his face, not caring if she was smothering him—he was just too fucking good at this and she wanted more. She arched her back with her hands pulling the ends of his hair while he drove her crazy with his tongue—in and out, in and out of her hot opening. She was reaching her peak, the warm shots of desire coming quicker as he continued to lick her to a dizzying frenzy, his dirty words humming into her. With one hand on her hip holding her steady and his head between her legs, his other hand travelled up to her breasts, cupping and squeezing one, then the other. He slid his hand underneath the blouse reaching her bare skin and they both heard a loud rip as the material tore and gave way. He looked up and she looked down.

"I'm sorry," he rasped, not sounding sorry at all, his lips and face glistening with her wetness.

"I'm not," she gasped breathlessly laughing, while pulling the shredded material completely off. "Keep going, baby," she urged, completely naked against the wall, and bringing his face back to her swollen, dripping skin. The look he gave her sent shivers through her. It was so lustful, his eyes dark and half closed. He gave an animalistic groan as his tongue lashed against her sensitive skin again with deft pressure and speed, one hand gripping her ass, with a finger running through her cheeks to the rhythm his tongue was moving. His other hand held her up by cupping a breast tightly and massaging. And thank the good lord she was anchored between him and the wall because the passionate onslaught all over her body was splintering her body apart. She came so hard and fast that she couldn't even feel her legs, crying out in pleasure as she pitched forward, collapsing onto him. He caught her, and lay on the carpet on his back with her on top of him. His hands moved hungrily over her back and hips as she caught her breath.

"Baby, that was amazing," she said lazily. "I think I might be done for the night." She leaned up to kiss him languidly and she felt his dick automatically push up into her. And he didn't stop, continuing to circle his hips against her and moaning against her lips. She loved hearing him start to lose control, and she felt her own need starting to build up again, even though she was dead tired.

"Kitten, I'm far from done. We need to make up for lost time." He spanked her ass sharply, making her jump. "Come on, up, on the bed, Sims. I need you. Don't make me come into a fucking towel again." His voice was gravelly and firm but she detected a hint of pleading. She pushed off of him and made her way to the bed, a silly grin on her face. He needed her.

"Well, when duty calls..." she sing-songed sweetly, and happily prepared herself for more of his sexual onslaught.

☙❧☙❧

He pushed his underwear off and when he came to the bed, she was already on her hands and knees, looking sexily over one shoulder at him, her eyes hooded, her wavy black hair a thick curtain hanging down to the mattress. The lips to her hot opening looked like moist petals to an inviting flower, beckoning him in, and he could still taste her on his tongue. She was so sexy, so erotic, that he wanted to burn an image of her like this into his brain. Would he ever get enough of her?

"Come to me," she commanded huskily. He quickly put on a condom and moved to her, teasing her by grazing his hard cock against her moist heat. Fuck she felt good. He gave a quick slap on that gorgeous ass of hers again, and she moaned low.

"How badly do you want it, baby?" he asked gruffly, trying to remain calm so he wouldn't lose it too quickly. He caressed the soft undersides of her ass cheeks with his hands, roving over to the top, right below her lower back to her ticklish spot. He wanted to hear those sweet squeals.

"I think we both know you're the one who needs it badly," she said teasingly, bursting into squealing giggles and pushing herself up against his engorged length. "Oh God, that's good," she moaned breathlessly. "Give it to me, baby," she pleaded, rubbing herself deliciously on his length. Her wetness left a glistening streak on his thighs, and Marc thought he was going to come from just that. Without waiting another second, he rammed himself into her, the force making her faceplant into the pillows, her whimpers muffled. He hissed, then paused to feel the exquisite suction of her muscles inside. He closed his eyes to try and relax himself because he didn't want to be too rough with her. He dragged her up on all fours again by her hips, then pulled his length almost all the way out, and back in deeply, doing it again and again as he took her from behind. Loud, grateful groans left her mouth every time, mingling with his own grunts as he took his fill, hitting all the right spots inside her, and fucking hell, it felt out of this world. He'd been waiting too long for her.

With one hand anchoring her by holding that sweet ass steady, he reached the other down to glide over her nipples as her full tits swayed, pinching the hardened tips. She shuddered. He kissed her back, his tongue dragging down her spine, and she arched and moaned. He moved a hand down to find her clitoris, pressing his index finger on that swollen bud, pushing her further to the edge. She whimpered long and loud, rocking her hips back into him. Her gold jewelry jangled as their bodies moved, their skin slapping stickily together and he picked up speed. Her sounds became higher pitched, and he knew she was close again. He flipped her to her back, wanting to see her face when they both came and grabbed both of her slender wrists over her head. He slid back inside and continued to pound into her as she bucked her hips to his. Then, he pulled back to watch himself move in and out of her moist opening. "Fuck, what a view," he groaned, as his eyes roamed over their joined bodies, his hard, hers soft. He couldn't believe he was connected to such a gorgeous goddess. Her eyes were closed, her thick liner smudged as she arched against him, her hands trapped in his and he felt a burst of possession just looking at her.

She was panting, "Yes, that's it. Take me *harder!*" He marveled at how verbal she was during sex, even bossy. He let go of her hands and bent down to kiss her because he just had to feel her words on his lips. She completely undid him. With his body on hers, he pumped into her more forcefully and her muscles tensed around his dick. She shuddered over and over again inside, squeezing him tight as she fell apart. The pleasure was so intense he thought he might pass out.

"Oh God, yes, *Marc!*" she cried, her voice filling the room loudly, her nails stinging down his back. He continued to move hard in and out of her, an arm under her ass to bring her closer to him, the other gripping a smooth leg around his torso. He felt the blood course through his body as he reached his pinnacle, his entire body stiffening as he finally came, coasting on his release. Her hands encouraged him, gently caressing his back as she softly murmured, "That's it, come to me, baby." And she continued to move with him, riding out her own pleasure.

He filled her with his hot liquid and his groan of release was just as loud as hers had been. He collapsed onto her, loudly muttering, "*Fuck yeah*, you're so good, kitten." His climax shook him. He had never had it so good as he had it with her. He captured her lips again, feeling her smile there, then rolled to the side pulling her with him, their slick bodies still joined and nestled together.

He brushed his fingers over that vulnerable spot on her neck, her pulse still fluttering quickly as she was coming down from her ecstasy high. He smiled in satisfaction and got up to clean himself off, his own pulse still racing, then returned to bed, nuzzling his head into her soft breasts. She was playing with his hair, stroking his ears. These moments were still new to him with a woman: the cuddling and closeness, just enjoying each other's company after their physical exertion. It was so much more intimate than even the dirtiest sex and never had he wanted to do this with anyone before. But with Simran, it was different. He wanted to stay in bed with her all day. There were moments when she had to remind *him* they both had to get up for other commitments.

He lightly glided his fingers over her, coming to the intricate gold of her necklace as it glowed in the dim light.

🙟🙟🙟

"Stop that, it tickles." She put her hand over his to still his curious one. He asked her where such beautiful things came from; did she buy them herself or receive them as gifts; were they from family or friends, or past lovers? She gave him a skeptical look and saw that he was actually serious. All right, she should have realized he would be full of questions as soon as she stepped out of that taxi in her sari. He was an inquisitive, well-rounded man, she already knew that. So why was she cautious about this subject?

"Lovers? Babe, we already know you're the one with a past harem, literally. I've only had just the eight lovers in my entire life, including you, and of those seven before you, well only one was really serious," she laughed nervously. She noticed his own deadpan stare, and a raised eyebrow, guessing that she was trying to skirt the topic. He really wanted to know? Ok then. She pushed the nervous feeling aside and set out to explain that it was a gift and a lot of it was cultural with an ultimate motive in mind.

"So, this was my mom's. It's special because her parents gave it to her and the matching earrings on her wedding day. My dad gifted both to me a few years ago when—" and she abruptly stopped. She almost told him about her bad break up, something she never talked about, keeping it tucked away in the furthest corner of her heart. She'd only ever just mentioned that one serious relationship to him in passing, when they first got back together a few weeks ago, but she didn't go into detail. He seemed to sense her hesitation and asked her to go on. "Well, that one involved relationship back in my twenties? We almost got engaged a few years back. He was a guy who worked for my dad in India," she said uncomfortably. He gasped in surprise. "And my dad gave me my mom's jewelry set around that time thinking my wedding was coming soon—that I would wear it on my special day. It didn't happen, so there's that. But," she continued, not letting him get in any questions about that painful time (he must have a shit ton now), "since I was little, jewelry, mainly gold, was always a common gift. Historically, it's supposed to be part of a woman's marriage dowry, and a form of security in case her husband turns out to be a dead beat. I mean, dowries aren't legal anymore in South Asia, but most people still believe in the tradition. I guess mine would be no different," she finished with a matter-of-fact tone, trying to move past the weird turn this conversation was taking. Did she just tell him about what could potentially be part of her dowry when she got married? *Crap.* They had just gotten together after London and marriage was so far from either of their minds. Wasn't it?

His face was masked, no emotion there for her to read, and he asked quietly if her family still believed in arranged marriages.

"Sure," she said airily, trying to keep the discussion light. "It's definitely a practice that still happens even amongst modern Indians. Remember my London friend, Tina? She and her husband were arranged, and it's working out pretty well. My dad is actually keeping his feelers out for me, hoping my perfect match is out there." She rolled her eyes, not bothering to hide the contempt in her voice at that last part. She didn't add that her dad was fully on the hunt for her future husband because she was now at a ripe age past thirty. Marc just kept his eyes fixated on her jewelry, remaining silent. *Say something,* she mentally urged him. Did she just freak the shit out of him?

❦❦❦

He felt something ugly twist his gut, something he was both familiar and unfamiliar with. The idea of marriage was unappealing to him, always had been since he'd been young. But what he wasn't used to, and even more fiercely unpleasant, was the thought of Simran with another man other than himself. He tried to move past it.

He cleared his throat. "So, is marriage really that important to you?" She was such an independent woman, and extremely driven in her career. He was the same way and truthfully satisfied with his way of life.

She gave him an alarmed look, then she relaxed while she contemplated. "Well, it's something I wouldn't *not* consider. In the South Asian culture, and amongst my family and friends, it's expected of me. But, I guess, outside of that, I expect it of me someday, too, along with a kid or two, one day," she said with honesty.

"Hmmm, really?" His tone was noncommittal while he stared from her intricately designed necklace to the flashing gold of her earrings. He'd never been one for marriage after witnessing his mom's experiences. The failed relationships, one after the other made him unsure of ever finding the one who would be there through thick and thin. And kids? He'd never even thought about actually ejaculating to create humans. He decided to change the subject. This conversation was starting to tread into dangerous territory. He pulled Simran into his arms and asked about her dad instead. He heard her exhale in relief, and he smiled at that; marriage wasn't something she wanted to talk about either.

She told him her father was amazing, but complicated. He moved her and her sister to Greenwich, CT, after their mom died of cancer. He wanted them to have access to all the opportunities that American kids had like the incredible education and freedom to choose what they wanted to be (to a certain degree). But they still had Indian nannies and an Indian housekeeper who doubled as their cook so that they had a taste of their first home. They also visited India annually, spending weeks at a time with relatives to always remember who and where they came from. Their father continued to live in Mumbai, managing his company, but still visited them monthly, because he wasn't one to shirk his fatherly duties. He doted on both girls, encouraging them to continue their studies and reach for their dreams. But even so, he was (and still is) old-fashioned about his daughters' futures and marriage—something she's struggled her whole life with him about and continues to do so. As for his career, her father started *Unified Entertainment Solutions* about thirty years ago. A company committed to servicing the Mumbai entertainment industry, then expanded to other markets globally.

"Wait a minute, your father *is* Kumar Khan?" Marc asked in disbelief. Startled, she answered yes. "Sims, I know of him. We worked with his company when we opened our club in Mumbai a few years ago." He gave a low whistle. "Wow, he's a shrewd, well-known businessman in his own right, and has incredible connections around the world."

Simran beamed with pride, laughing a little. "Yeah, he has his good points."

Then she curiously asked about his father because she knew some about his mom raising him alone. He told her candidly that his dad freaked out when he was a baby, leaving them on their own. He never returned and Marc never knew him. He wasn't so sure he ever wanted to, either. Simran nodded, holding him close as she empathized with losing a parent early in life. He continued, explaining that his childhood was pretty great, despite everything. His mom didn't have much, but she gave him love, kindness and acted as both parents as much as she could. His grandparents were also in the picture before they passed away, giving him a great foundation. The hardest part had been growing up watching his mom go through a slew of boyfriends. They weren't always the nicest guys and didn't treat her with respect. All of that's behind her now, and she's happy with herself. She's currently retired and concentrating on her pottery, living in a house he bought for her in Santa Barbara. He visits as often as he can find the time to given his busy work schedule. The absent father figure, though, that always felt like a missing puzzle piece to him, especially as a teenager and while in college. As an adult, he was able to let it go, but he wasn't so sure about ever delving into fatherhood because of it.

59

Chapter 17

The smell of steak wafted through the air as Simran stepped out of the bathroom, making her mouth water. Her annoying stomach gurgled again, and Marc tried to hide his smile. She ignored him and went to the chair he offered her.

Her hair was still up in a hasty bun, and she'd donned a cozy, grey lounge-wear sweater, and matching wide leg pants. She felt refreshed from her shower and hoped she looked better, given the circumstances.

Marc crossed to the other side of the table and sat down. He gave her a once over then smiled tenderly. "You look lovely, Simran." His voice was warm and genuine. "Do you feel better?"

She tried to swallow past the emotions welling inside her throat again. Damn him and his charming ways. She only nodded and gave him what she hoped was a smooth smile back, when inside she was all turmoil.

"Well dig in," he said with gusto. "Chef makes a juicy steak here, you'll love it." The broad grin on his roguishly handsome face took Simran's breath away. He was so adorable in his enthusiasm for life's pleasures.

Sighing, she took a bite of her steak. "Delicious," she agreed. They ate in silence, him serving her a helping of the spinach and potatoes.

After a few minutes, he asked, "Simran, would you have ever told me about the baby if it had lived?" There was a softness in his voice, knowing he was treading on dangerous territory. She stopped eating and took a sip of sparkling water, complete with lemon slice. That was the way she liked it and knew Marcus had thoughtfully put it in for her. She was getting all mixed up in her feelings for him now and where she stood about them. He'd stayed to make sure she was ok and that she was fed. And now he wanted to talk about the pregnancy. He had every right to ask her about it, but she felt blindsided, like the rug was being pulled out from under her that he even wanted to. It was obvious he still cared.

"To be honest, Marcus, I don't know. I didn't get that far." She saw his gorgeous mouth turn down and she knew he didn't want to hear that. But being pregnant had left little room to think about more than herself and the safety of the baby. Her mind was still whirling from the fact that she was growing a life, and her impending new role as a single mother. She hadn't yet planned for when the baby actually arrived and what upbring they would have. "Would you have really wanted to be a dad? Given what we talked about that one night after the Indian wedding?" She felt her cheeks heat up as she remembered the events leading up to that conversation. After they had passionately taken what they wanted from each other's bodies, a discussion came up that was both eye-opening and awkward. It hadn't been too in-depth, but it was something that stuck with her. Marc didn't want kids, and marriage was not his end game. The marriage part actually hadn't bothered her as much as the parenthood part did. She had always seen herself as a mom one day.

"I don't know, maybe." He shook his head and sat back in his chair. *What!?* Simran was stunned by his answer but tried to hide it. The wheels were churning in his head, she could almost see them. His hand went through his thick locks anxiously again, finally saying low and gruff, "Actually, a lot of folks don't know they want to become parents until they're up against it. I think I would have been ok with it, Sims." Despite his anxiety, he seemed pretty calm when he said that. He reached for her hand, holding it across the table, rubbing his thumb back and forth over the top. She shivered at his use of her nickname; the one she so secretly loved. He held her eyes with his own gaze, and she was taken aback by the truthfulness there. *Oh, good grief!* Now she was really confused. Would he have felt this way if she had told him back then? She would never know. Instead of dwelling on that, she curled her fingers over his, holding his hand back while they sat in silence.

Marcus looked at the clock. "It's late. I should let you get some sleep." He got up and walked around to her side of the table. She was done eating and started to get up, too. He helped her to stand then hugged her, and she let him this time. Without heels, she came to his shoulders, and he leaned his tall form down to rest his chin on the top of her head. She marveled at how they fit so perfectly, even with the height difference. She heard him take a long inhale and smiled to herself. *Me, too, Marc.* His scent filled her nostrils pleasantly again, and she knew she would never be able to get enough of it. She heard his sigh and then he disentangled himself from her.

While he gathered his things, she awkwardly asked if she had dreamt it, or had he massaged her while she slept. Turning toward her hesitantly, an unsure lift to his lips, he answered, "Yeah, that was me. You seemed so uncomfortable, and you needed your rest. I thought I would help you out, and I wanted to," he added, as she started to tell him he didn't need to do it. She smiled gratefully and thanked him. "You're welcome," he answered, and they stood looking at each other for a beat.

He moved to call the concierge and have someone remove the used platters and plates, then cleared his throat. "Simran, I'm right upstairs in the Frederick suite. if you need anything, ok?" he said at the door. She smiled a little sadly at him and nodded yes, coming to him.

He gave her a soft, lingering kiss on the cheek before he left, and she didn't move away, wanting to remember this moment. She didn't tell him that she didn't want to know about where his room was, and she didn't want to need him for anything.

Simran realized it wasn't as easy as all that as she closed the door on his retreating figure. For fuck's sake, if only she could just close the door to her feelings for him, too. She'd been so resolute before today, but after seeing him and everything that transpired in the past few hours, things seemed to be turning on their head.

A trace of his musk and fresh mint scent still lingered in the room, and that familiar hollow feeling in her chest she thought was gone for good had returned. She truly missed him again. The thing was, she thought as she went to lay down, pulling the covers back this time and fluffing her pillow, who could say if he had really changed or not? His playboy existence seemed more than satisfactory to him right up until they'd met, and he appeared to enjoy the jet setting lifestyle immensely. Not only did they happen to run into a few of his past glamourous girlfriends in person (how could they not while in London and then NYC), but she looked up some of his past affairs online after her warning conversation with Tina early on in their relationship. It was agonizing but she needed to know. It took a while to find anything except career highs and philanthropic accolades. His escapades seemed to barely exist for the past three to four years, even though she knew better. But when she finally did find some recent articles, and perused the older ones, she briefly registered that every single woman was either an actress, model, or an heiress of some kind or another. Women who were confident in the limelight and fed off of Marc's sexual prowess and jet-setting lifestyle. Not to say that she wasn't confident herself, but she realized she was in a whole different category than these women. How could she measure up to what he was used to? And then on the flip side, *was* she so dissimilar from them? Would he discard her, too, when he got tired of what they had?

But now, after months of separation, maybe he *had* changed and was trying to tell her that. Had she broken through a barrier he'd always kept closely guarded? She didn't think it was possible, but her mind ruminated. She recalled a specific encounter, when they ran into a past fling of his in NYC, and how they had both reacted. She herself had been so affected by it, so filled with jealousy, rage, and her own self worthlessness in the face of a lifestyle that was unknown to her, that she almost couldn't see straight. And what had he done? He'd been astounded and upset about her distress and did everything he could to quell her fears. There were some signs there, she had to admit...

೧೧೧೧

THREE MONTHS AGO

"You ready?" Simran asked, stepping out of her bedroom while fastening large, skinny gold hoop earrings into her ears. She smoothed the high ponytail at the crown of her head and checked her makeup one last time in her compact before snapping it shut and throwing it into her purse.

Marc was lounging on her couch, long legs stretched out in front of him, flipping through one of her design books. She had to admit he looked almost too large for her modest West Village abode, but he seemed so comfortable as if he fit right in. At the moment, he was perusing a catalog of interior focal points from the early twentieth century, having gleefully discovered her wide collection of historical architectural digests a few weeks ago. He really was an adorably sexy nerd. And he was hers, she thought a little smugly.

"Yeah," he answered absentmindedly then looked up at her. His eyes got wide, and he let out a low wolf whistle. "Come here," he commanded, a slow sexy smile coming to his lips.

"What?" she said, turning this way and then the other, inspecting herself. Had she gotten a stain on the suede of her red mini skirt?

"Just, I need to see you better," he said impatiently, reaching a hand out to her. She came over to him and took it. He pulled her to stand between his legs and his warm hands moved up the sides of her knees, then high on her thighs where the hem of her skirt ended. His fingers fiddled with the material, tickling her then moved underneath to caress her bare skin. Simran shivered and closed her eyes in delight. His eyes swept up from her black mid-calf boots with the red thunderbolt design, to her mini skirt, and finally to her sheer, black mohair sweater with her black bondage style bra purposefully showing through. "Wow, baby. I don't think we're going to make it on time," he continued with mock disappointment, his voice low, his eyes focused on her breasts, trying to undo the lacing with laser focus. His hands crept up her bare ass cheeks and grazed the tiny material of her thong before giving her bottom a squeeze. "Shit, kitten, such sweet cheeks," he whispered deep and gravelly.

Simran felt the heat from his look slide over her body; felt his hands squeeze her, and she knew they were going to lose it if she didn't act fast. She chuckled huskily, putting her hands on his shoulders, trying to tamp down the small waves of desire starting to roll inside her before they became a typhoid of lust that only he could control. In all honesty, she should be annoyed because this was becoming a habit. He wanted to undress everything she had carefully put together, not being able to wait until after they got back. And she was annoyed, but she was also secretly pleased at his uncontrollable passion for her.

"Babe, we need to go. This is important," she said, trying to keep her voice firm.

"Are you sure?" he asked, while slowly motorboating his face into her breasts. *Oh God, so good.*

"Marc!" she batted his face away. She took in his simple outfit of faded black jeans and heather grey crewneck shirt—which only accentuated his wide, muscular chest and ripped arms—and brown leather, custom Chuck Taylor-like high tops from Prada (the man knew what he liked) and tried to shake her head in disgust. Men would never get what women had to go through for style, but she had to admit he looked good enough to eat—something she planned to do later with him, she thought darkly. She cleared her throat. Oh, for fuck's sake, the man was turning her into a legit sex addict. She was horny for him all the freaking time, and constantly ruining her underwear.

He looked up at her, noticing how hard it was for her to breathe. "You sure I can't help you out there, sweetie?" he asked, while she moved away laughing. "How about letting me taste some of that brown sugar?" His hands were trying to reach for her again. Oh God, he made things sounds so filthy.

That devastatingly devilish smile was spreading across his mouth and blond locks were falling onto his forehead. He was utterly roguish.

"You're the devil in foxy, hot man clothes," she said over her shoulder, moving toward the door. She batted her eyelashes at him. "I promise it'll be so much better if we wait, babe."

"I'm holding you to that promise, baby," he replied, grabbing his wallet and keys, and following her out into the hallway. He stopped right in front of her but didn't touch her, and she was forced to tilt her head back to look up at him. "You know the devil always remembers a pact." His tone was a little dangerous but his eyebrows wiggled comically and his eyes were twinkling. Then he turned to lead the way to the elevator. She took in the sight of his tight ass in those "casual" jeans, and she swallowed hard, tamping down her lust.

"Mhm," was all she could manage with a secretive smile. He was so addictive. One of them had to have a little control, didn't they?

꼱꼱꼱

They arrived at the gallery opening in Chelsea that mid-summer evening to an enthusiastic crowd. The space was filled with tasteful, art deco inspired sculptures, composed of differing metals that simultaneously complemented and juxtaposed together. Marc had been talking about this event for days, raving about how hard the artist worked. Coming from a broken community, he'd been through hell and high water to get his artwork out there. Marc felt for him and was in the midst of brainstorming a philanthropic-type venture where he funded all the costs associated for an artist to get their work out to the public so they could concentrate on just their craft. The artist they were seeing today was his inspiration. The emphasis would be on those from broken communities or upturned family situations (Marc having first-hand experience with this) to give them a leg up for success. The details came to culmination as Simran and Marcus whispered excitedly to each other while riding the subway to the opening. Taking the subway was Simran's idea. Marc admitted recently that public transportation hadn't been his mode for getting around in a long time, to Simran's horror. She wanted him to experience NY's inspiring blood, sweat, and tears up close and personal.

They were enjoying themselves when they arrived, mingling and chatting. Marc was a social butterfly as he eagerly praised the artist, a circle of admirers (for both the artist *and* Marc) hovering around them. He kept Simran close, an arm around her waist and a warm hand pressed firmly—maybe even a little possessively—on her hip while he held court and, honestly, she didn't mind one bit. She looked up at him, saw his handsome face split into laughter at something the artist said, and she melted, like she always did. Was he it for her?

All of a sudden they heard a high-pitched squeal from across the room, reminiscent of a cat getting its tail squashed. A very tall blonde came tottering to Marc, ignoring Simran completely. Almost a good head taller than him in her sky-high stilettos, she bent down to cuddle into his other side, exposing her chest in the process. He smiled in recognition, pulling her in for a hug while letting go of Simran. The frigidness of suddenly not being held by Marc, combined with the boiling heat in her head at the gall of this woman made Simran a bit woozy. *Keep it together, Simran.* This wasn't the first time something like this had happened.

"Cressida," he said warmly, "wow, I thought you were on a modeling tour in Eastern Europe for the better part of this year." He pecked her briefly on the cheek, followed by trying to unwind her octopus like arms from around him. He automatically reached for Simran, but she had physically stepped away, needing a minute to sort her warring emotions. He looked around and found her, his brows furrowed, eyes questioning. Simran ignored him and stood quietly by.

"I just got back," Cressida cooed in a high voice, straw-colored bangs falling into squinty eyes. "And I'm so looking forward to picking up where we left off," she followed in a voice about three octaves lower, her arms encircling Marc again. Simran would have laughed at that if she hadn't been so irate. Despite already happening a handful of times (was she invisible or something?), she still wasn't used to this. The insecure feeling that she was the same to him—nothing but a short-term fling—kept flitting through her mind, whittling at her assurance.

"Cressida, let me introduce you to Simran. We're here together," he said while simultaneously pulling Cressida's long arms from his waist again. He reached for Simran, pulling her close to his side, and suddenly, her doubts disappeared. *Jeez, was she bi-polar?* Pasting a smile on her face, she looked up at the tall gazelle, noticing that her eyes were not on an even level, but she was quite startlingly attractive in an all angles and lines sort of way.

"Nice to meet you, Cressida," Simran said politely.

"Oh," Cressida said, disappointedly, the hostility an undercurrent. "Wow, you're so exotic. Where did Marky find you?" she asked, fingering Marc's hair a little too familiarly. Simran's eyes crossed a bit at the word 'exotic' and this time she knew that boiling sensation would bubble over as she watched that beanpole touch Marc.

Marc interjected, obviously seeing Simran's face contort into disgust. Oh, he better step in. He knew her well. She would give this Cressida woman an earful, probably wasting her breath, too, because this bimbo had air where her brain should be.

"We met in London, Cressida. Simran's a New Yorker, but her family is Indian." He looked down at Simran with utter adoration, squeezing her hip. He was trying to calm her down. Kudos to him, and definitely an out of this world blow-job tonight as a reward, she thought warmly, looking up at him.

"Oh," Cressida answered, awe in her tone. Then she genuinely asked, "Dot or Feather?" Marc's eyes became round saucers and he tried to recover by laughing embarrassingly. Simran choked on her drink, coughing while Marc whacked her back.

"Say what now?" she finally managed when she could take a clear breath again. Had she heard correctly?

"*Dot* or *feather*?" Cressida emphasized slowly, arcing her arm so that champagne sloshed onto the floor, just missing Simran's red skirt.

"Dot actually, and wow, thanks for asking," Simran said dryly. She could feel the heat creeping up her chest, neck, and into her face. Was steam coming out of her burning ears now? *Aak!* she needed to get the hell out of there before she blew. "Nice to meet you, Cressida, is it?" She pushed her glass at Marc, turned on her heel and left.

The fresh air, even with the rank sour and sweet undercurrent from the piled garbage bags curbside, felt better than the stifling hot and cold she felt in the gallery. Honestly, what was the matter with her? Marc was with her, and these other women were in his past now. But that twat in there would have suffered a major head butt, forcing her eyes to sit on level if Simran hadn't left.

She saw a lone smoker outside, and thanked God above that there were those who still fed into their nicotine habits the old-fashioned way. She quit many years ago, but right now, the need was dire. The ritual of paper tip to mouth, inhale, then exhale was eating at her. She asked the man if she could bum one. Looking her up and down, he happily obliged.

"Thanks," she said while he lit her tip with his. As she took her first inhale in a long time, the nicotine quickly hit her system, calming her nerves. "Ahh, sweet nicotine, I worship at your feet," she said to no one in particular, a little light-headed. The gentleman outside chuckled and sidled closer to her, his shoulder brushing hers.

"So, you have a name, beautiful?" he asked, leaning into her. Before she could answer, Marc came flying out looking for her, the look of worry on his handsome face would have liquefied her if she hadn't been so rankled by that Bambi in there.

"Simran!? Sims!? Jesus, come on, why did you leave? Listen—" he cut off, seeing her, "—what the fuck? You don't smoke!" he said in confusion, his eyes large and round again.

"Hey, man, she's fine. We're just enjoying each other's company," the other gentleman said, trying to claim her attention back.

"It's ok, I'm with this guy," Simran said to her new friend, waving her hand in Marc's direction. "Although sometimes I wonder what I'm doing," she continued under her breath. She noticed Marc's nostrils flared and jaw clenching while he registered the other man outside with her. Good, let him see how it felt. She turned back to the unknown guy, giving him her brightest smile, which felt entirely fake, and completely ignored Marc. "I do have a name it's—"

Marc came up behind her, grabbing her arm, pulling her aside to talk with some privacy. "Don't," she snapped, jerking away. She looked at him defiantly as she took one more inhale, trying not to choke as her lungs tried to find their way around the smoke. Her glare dared him to comment on how bad she was being (she'd heard it from everyone in the past, so why not him, too). His bright eyes flashed dangerously. Stubbing out the cigarette with the heel of her favorite boots, she turned back to him. "You know, I just needed to calm my nerves and the alcohol *wasn't* cutting it," she seethed and turned to leave. He caught her arm again, holding tightly this time, and glowered at her.

"Baby, I don't care if you have an occasional smoke. Shit, smoke all the tobacco in the tri-state area, but give me a chance to explain who that was," he growled, then his look softened when he saw the distress on her face. "She's no one to me. We were together—"

"*Really?* Do I need to hear more about your many, *many* past women...again? You think I *enjoy* hearing about each and every one of them?" she laughed angrily. She was furious. Her cheeks were hot again, her breasts heaving in her sheer sweater, over her racy bondage-style bra. She saw his eyes roam down her body, and she knew he couldn't help it. She was absolutely turned on right now, too, inexplicably so. That's what he did to her: made her crazy with lust when she should want to knock him over the head with a frying pan.

∽∽∽∽

"*Fu-ugh!*" she grumbled loudly and flounced away, her high ponytail swinging in the air. "Sorry!" she apologized to the lone smoker. Then she was gone, strutting down Tenth Avenue in her red mini skirt and rocker-style boots, looking like a hot, modern go-go dancer. Christ, she was sexy, and fucking exasperating, Marc thought, watching her ass shake as she left. The unknown man coughed uncomfortably. He turned from the view of Simran's amazing backside to glance over to him, cocking an eyebrow.

"May I help you?" Marc asked sardonically.

The guy was giving him a "go the fuck after her" kind of look. "No, man, just, I would *not* let that one get away." Marc grunted in agreement and followed her.

"Fu-ugh?" he asked her softly when he caught up with her.

"Don't start with me," she said testily. "I couldn't decide if this was a 'Fuck' or an 'Ugh' situation." She continued to march away. Marc pursed his lips, trying not to laugh. "You know, babe," she went on, stomping down Tenth Avenue, fiddling in her purse, "if I'm being honest, you were a slut in your past life. That's not what my main problem is, though. I'm just having a hard time seeing you, this amazing, intellectual man, with all of these empty-headed women. I mean, what did they offer you besides sex?" She shook out a tic-tac and popped it in her mouth. "But the thing is, they're all absolutely stunning, they totally fit in with your lifestyle. Then I start to wonder what the hell you're doing with me. Are we also doing this whirlwind fling? Is that what you expect from this?"

All laughter was gone from Marc as he listened to her, and a heat spread inside his chest. Her praise for him always did that. But he also felt helpless, and that spreading heat started to take the form of a knot. Here was this incredible woman, *his* woman, who felt low because of him and his past. She had nothing to do with what he had been like before, and those other women? They were nothing in comparison to this warm, beautiful, intelligent goddess. He didn't know why she couldn't see that. And he wanted only her. She was the whole package, and he had no interest in letting her go or horsing around. He let her fume as they tried to hail a cab back to his place, as was their usual custom for the night. Frustrated, she threw up her hands and told him to come back to hers which was only a few blocks away.

They walked off her anger rather than take the subway. And as they walked, her litany of annoyances continued, including how racist that Crest Toothpaste of a woman was, spitting out the name like a bug caught in her mouth. Then questioning how they always went to his place at night. What was he, the boss of their relationship? She stormed to no one in particular. He would have laughed at the absurdity of it all if she wasn't so tightly wound.

When they got back to her place, really only a fifteen-minute walk from the gallery, she was calmer, and her self-assurance returned enough to have her way with him. She warned him, as she flicked on some music on her sound system, that she was still irritated and was now going to dole out his punishment. By that, she meant he had to sit back and watch her undress completely, not letting him lift a finger to help or touch her. This was the worst kind of punishment for Marc to endure and she knew it. Simran was fully aware of his impatience when it came to their physical play.

The tinkling of piano keys filled the room, followed by quirky synthesizer pings and a woman's throaty voice. Soft, but deep, bass beats filtered in as the woman started to sing about not seeing anybody around, so she proceeds to feel herself. Marc was stunned as he watched Simran undress. She made everything dirty by elongating and deliberating all of her movements. At the same time, with a sexy half smile on her lips, she educated him about what they were listening to – "Scuse Me," by Lizzo—a song about female empowerment and self-love. It would play on repeat until she was done with what she was doing. He was aroused and slack-jawed at what he was about to view. When she bent over to take off those boots, shaking to the sensual and quirky beat of the music, he got a full view of those smooth ass cheeks and the slightest material of her underwear covering her pussy. He was riveted. But fuck, he wanted to feel her smooth skin so badly, wanted his mouth on her breasts, needed her body wrapped around his, especially after the flux of emotions that had pushed and pulled both of them that evening. He tried to reason with her, but she wasn't having it. He couldn't help unbuttoning his jeans while he took a seat on her couch to fist his own hardening cock, when she finally unlaced that bondage style bra and threw it at his feet. Her black thong followed shortly after, hitting him square in the chest when she snapped it at him sling-shot style. He grabbed the barely-there material, feeling her wetness on it and put it up to his nose, inhaling deeply, his eyes still on her. Her face heated up in embarrassment, while she swayed into her bedroom completely naked to lay back on the bed and she paused. He followed her leaning against the wall, his hands openly down his pants, and he asked if he could join her now. She gave him a stern look and shook her head. He rasped for her to go on then, with whatever she had in mind, as it dawned on him that she was going to touch herself, too, while he watched on. She smiled and wordlessly continued with her game. She cupped her own breasts, sliding her palms over her dark nipples, and circling them to sharp nibs. She moaned at the sensation; her eyes half closed. One hand stayed on her breast while the other slid down between her legs. She spread her smooth, coppery thighs and from where he was standing, he could see every bit of her sweet skin as it glistened wet while her fingers slid over and through the lips of her perfect pussy. Marc was breathing heavily now, audible to both their ears. He wanted to be a part of her sexual play so badly and began to move to her, but she halted him with a hand up, taunting huskily that he should relax and enjoy the performance. With a groan, he withdrew back while she continued her self-care and his excruciating torture. He couldn't stop his appreciative growls and words of encouragement, as he moved his hand back and forth along his rock-hard length in response to her erotic display. He honestly thought he was going to burst. Then something changed in her movements. She became wilder and he realized that his hungry stare, watching every move she made to herself, was not only turning her on, but making her lose control. She fingered and rubbed herself with such a frenzy that her body bucked, and she came so hard she screamed at the pleasure, calling out his name. Still in a haze, her skin deliciously flushed, she finally allowed him to join her. She murmured throatily that it was his turn now and with hooded dark eyes, she pushed him back onto the mattress. Shoving his pants down, she set her luscious lips on his engorged dick and proceeded to work him hard, giving him a blow-job so intense that it rocked his world inside out. He thought he died from the pleasure of her warm mouth sucking him, in just the right way, making him buck and come in the same wild energy she had a few moments ago. The sex that followed was well worth the wait; intense, hot and rough with their emotions wrangling out of their writhing bodies.

And how had he calmed her down before her uninhibitedly fucking hot show? He embraced her as they walked to her apartment, and just held her on each and every block corner as they waited for the walk signals, stroking her rigid back. He whispered in her ear everything he thought about her. Things like, "You are so fucking gorgeous and smart," "I only want you and only you," "I want to kiss your sassy mouth all damn day," "I really love your peaches, want to shake your tree," until her stance relaxed, and the giggles bubbled out of her. She slapped his chest and called him a joker a la her favorite Steve Miller Band song which he'd just quoted, and he was relieved he could make her smile again. He cared for this woman so much, and it wounded him that she was hurt. What dumbfounded him the most was that he could even feel this way about another person.

Chapter 18

That day for her, had signified a change in their relationship. *Relationship*, even the word made Simran cringe, her mind filtering back to the present. But he made her feel so comfortable, so confident in her own skin that a man like him would deign to be with her; an everyday woman just trying to make her way; someone who enjoyed public transportation and the challenge of creating her own modest business. Sure, her family had some money, but not like what he was now accustomed to with his affluent way of life. But she really thought they had something. She dared to hope that she didn't have bad luck when it came to relationships. A thought that had been a constant companion since her world had been torn apart by heartbreak six years ago.

That scenario had been with someone she thought she could trust, someone she believed wanted her beyond a doubt and forever. She'd been misled, partly because she was still finding her own footing as a young woman, and also because the situation pleased her father. She didn't have feelings for this man anymore, wasn't even sure if she could call what they had love, but her self-assurance had been shaken. And she still conflictingly felt the need to please her father, even if what he wanted and she wanted were on opposite spectrums. She would always feel that need to be the good Indian daughter.

As if on cue, her phone rang, and it was her dad. He was never good with the nine and a half hour time difference between Mumbai and NYC. She squinted at the clock. What time was it? She'd been up all night with her thoughts. The clock winked back eleven in the evening here, so it was around half past eight the next morning over there. He must be just leaving for work.

"Hi, *Abba* (dad)," she said over the phone, her tone unsure, her energy jittery. Her father had mood swings like no other, except for Sabine, a trait she inherited from him.

"Sima! *Beta* (kiddo), how are you?" his boisterous voice called over the line. "Bina said you were sick for a while. How are you? Are you taking your vitamins?" He continued without letting her answer, "What about that herb supplement I brought you from my doctor last time?" He was referring to some health tincture or other that his "doctor" (really what they would call a quack in the US) had provided him and he gave to her and her sister the last time he was in town.

"*Jee* (yes), *Abba*. I'm taking my vitamins and I was *still* sick. But I feel ok now. I think it may have been a stomach bug that was going around. I was pretty busy with work, too, so I couldn't rest as well as I should have," she lied. It came out so naturally it felt almost real. There were things she could never tell her father (it all came with the 'straddling two cultures' territory) like the fact that she had accidentally gotten knocked up (let alone the fact that she was sexually active; could *any* daughter really ever admit that to their dad?). Or that she had miscarried. Even the major detail that she'd been seeing Marc, not to mention any of her love-life as a grown woman. Her cancer situation, though, that she would talk to him about, but she would wait until her test results came back. Her father still got emotional when he thought about her mother's passing from stomach cancer over twenty years ago.

"*Aacha* (fine). I was so worried," he screamed over the phone, even though they both had a great connection. "So, I talked to Anil yesterday." *Here we go again.* This was an on-going conversation they'd had been dancing around for the past few years. More recently, it was the emphasis every time they talked. Simran knew it had to do with some of the local Aunties' gossiping to her father about Marc from last summer. He wasn't explicit, but he hadn't been pleased over the phone during one chat, saying he couldn't believe the yucky reputations of some of these American men who thought they were a great catch. Simran understood then, without a doubt, that her father knew. For him, culture and family were ingrained, and it was crucial that they continue with his children. It didn't matter if she dated a saint. If he wasn't Indian, he got an automatic ding.

"Oh yeah?" she said noncommittedly, trying her hardest to will the topic to go away.

"*Jee.* He's agreed to meet you when you come for a visit next week. You are still coming to Mumbai, are you not? His parents very much want to see you, too, to make sure things are—" he broke off to suck his teeth trying to find the right words, "—all right between you and Anil."

She gave a great big sigh, absolutely audible to her dad over the phone. But he went on. "Sima, *beta*, you know this is the right thing. How can I take care of your future if you won't listen to me?" he asked, his frustration making its debut for the evening, causing his voice to go a few octaves higher. Fatherly duties were also culturally deep-rooted in him, even though his daughters were independent women who could take care of themselves. Like many South Asian men of his generation, he still felt the responsibility to make sure they were taken care of, married, and with children, before he left this life.

"*Abba*, seriously? I can't believe you're still stuck on this. Anil and I broke up six years ago. The guy left *me*, remember? He stomped all over my heart and left me to hang out with some German chick while in Munich for work." She paused, realizing the irony of how that situation had kind of replayed itself out with Marc, minus the German chick part. Man, she was water and relationships were oil. There was no way the two could mix no matter what she did. "He was working for you at the time ... does that ring a bell? He and I have nothing in common now, and I've completely moved on. Why don't you worry more about how my *business* is doing? I'm doing great by the way. I made The Knot's 2020 vendor list, and you know that's one of the best achievements in my industry. Everyone refers to that list in search of the best, most influential vendors..." Hope flooded her voice. She would always have that South Asian child angst of wanting to please her parents, no matter what age she was or how successful she became.

"*Thicke ache* (all right), that's good to hear," he said, with sincerity. She could almost envision his South Asian head bob while he spoke, not quite a nod, not quite a shake. She knew the approval washing over her would be short-live, though. "What do you mean you have nothing in common with Anil? Aren't you both smart, good-looking, and have business degrees? You know he is like a son to me and will take care of the family business and *all* of you, even your *kharap* (bad) sister. He is perfect for you, Sima. He just needed some time to explore himself. You know how men can be. Even I know how men can be," he chortled. "He didn't get the opportunity you had growing up in America." And now he was hitting her with what conflicted her the most about her life: South Asian guilt, where loyalty, and obedience were expected of children toward their parents and elders. Decisions were made for said children because it was in the family's best interest. Simran didn't want this heavy weight on her shoulders and yet, it was being foisted on her without any discussion, to a person who had wrecked her trust many years. She knew this situation would literally make or break her happiness.

"Dad," she said, cutting the niceties, getting his attention with her use of the non-Indian word for father, which he hated (he wanted his kids to remain as Indian as possible, even with their American lifestyle). "If he's like a son to you, wouldn't that make him my *brother*?" She knew she was being juvenile and didn't know how many times she'd played this card, maybe a thousand times?

He sucked his teeth sharply again, this time in aggravation. "Do *not* be smart with me, Simran. I raised you to respect your elders," he chided her over the phone. "I am not taking no for an answer. You will be on that plane next week to meet with Anil. Remember your family duty," he said firmly, and then hung up, his emotions getting the best of him. There was that guilt again. What did she expect? Her dad was the patriarch of their family to the nth degree, him being the eldest and most successful of his siblings and in-laws. He always got the results he wanted and everyone in his sphere was like a pawn in his own little game of chess. It only fueled his arrogance. Again, she was hit with irony because that characteristic in Marc, the part that had first attracted her to him, was his arrogance.

"Great catching up with you too, *Abba*," Simran said to no one.

Chapter 19

The next morning, Marcus got up early and hit the gym. He hadn't slept well, tossing and turning all night from yesterday's events. Simran and everything she'd been through took over his brain and he'd stared listlessly at the ceiling for hours at one point. He hit the gym anyway, taking his frustrations out on the weights and treadmill, listening to Led Zeppelin's *House of the Holy* album to energize him and keep his focus.

He came back to his suite and showered afterward. He ordered room service for breakfast and reviewed some last-minute contracts before his full day of meetings. After dressing, he headed down to the nineteenth floor to Simran's room. He noticed the "Do Not Disturb" sign on her door but knocked anyway. No one answered. He tried again and called her name. Still no answer. Fine. He would leave her alone right now. It was early and she was probably sleeping. He would try again later. He was determined to work this out with her somehow and help her with whatever she needed.

He spent the first part of the day in midtown with investors, reviewing the initial financing to revamp a flailing European style night club in Queens. He emailed follow-up notes to Bruce who was still in Vancouver for a few more days finishing up with that shit storm there. Then he hopped down to the Lower East Side to scope out the renovations on his 'gallery in the sky' project. He really wished Simran was with him, not only to walk through the finished product, but just so she could share in the excitement. She helped him carve out the idea and now it was taking shape. She was a part of it.

Once stepping through the twenty-fifth-floor penthouse space, though, he knew she'd done an impeccable job in overseeing it, following his directions, and even making her own contributions to the space. The floor to ceiling windows felt like they were walking in the urban sky. In fact, the sky itself would be an absolute dream in all of its stages of differing hues from morning until night; a natural light show bouncing off the mirrored skyscrapers. The interior of the room itself was kept simple, with blond hardwood floors, and the sectional walls breaking up the space were done up in a dark green, almost black, marble pattern shot with veins of gold. It was stark but elegant and he couldn't wait to get the artists' work inside.

Afterwards, he met with curators to talk about the next steps. Halfway through the meeting, his brain started to blur. His mind returned to Simran again and he really had trouble keeping his head in the game. Instead of trying to push thoughts of her aside, like he had in Vancouver, he cut the meeting short and rescheduled for another day. He had more pressing matters he wanted to take care of.

He got back to the hotel in the late afternoon and headed to her suite. He found the housekeeping staff there, pulling sheets off the bedding, dumping out the trash bins, their Latin music quietly playing in the background on one of their devices. None of Simran's things were in sight.

"Excuse me, but do you know if this guest already checked out?" he asked one of them. They just shrugged their shoulders and turned back to finish their task. *Shit, shit, shit.* He'd been too confident and too cocky thinking he was making headway with her. He texted her, hoping she would answer him quickly. Fifteen minutes later and with no response, he tried a different method.

Running his hand down his face and through his hair, he made his way to the concierge desk. He didn't see Sabine, so he had her paged. After a few minutes, she appeared, wearing a fitted black suit, both pin and glasses glinting in the light, and she looked ready to do war with him.

Clasping her hands in front of her, she calmy asked, "How may I help you today, Mr. Lehigh?" He was beyond frustrated but tried to remain calm.

"Where is she, Sabine?" he demanded. She closed her eyes condescendingly and then opened them, showing her annoyance.

"I'm not at liberty to divulge other client's personal information," she answered with a bland smile.

"Come on!" he barked, slapping his hand on the marble counter. It stung, but he didn't care. "I'm here to make things right. I need to know where she is. We're not through talking." It wasn't his finest moment. Usually, he could remain cool and collected, but right now his emotions were getting the best of him, and he didn't give a shit.

Sabine sucked in a deep breath through her nose and let it out slowly from her mouth. Then she leaned her upper body toward him, meeting him almost eye to eye in her lofty heels. Pointing a long, manicured finger in his face, she quietly, but forcefully whispered, "You fucked up, Mr. Lehigh. You don't deserve her. If you weren't one of our top billing clients, I would have your ass kicked out of here." She straightened back up and cleared her throat, smoothing her suit jacket down. He knew Sabine was over-protective of Simran and had been since their mother passed when they were kids. Family was so important to them. So, it wasn't too much of a shock when she came at him like this. He admired her protectiveness, but he needed to find Simran.

"Sabine…" he said giving her a warning look. Pinching her lips, she closed her eyes dramatically again. When she opened them, her anger was replaced with black ice.

"I know you're not an idiot, Mr. Lehigh. In fact, quite the opposite, I hear. Given that Simran *lives* in Manhattan, and *isn't* here in the hotel, one can only guess where she could be." Her eyebrows arched high, her hands in the air as she shrugged. "Good evening." She left this statement hanging in the air and turned on her heel, walking back to her office.

Clearly he wasn't thinking straight; of course, she would be at her apartment. Was this the right thing for him to do? The push and pull of all these emotions flooded heavily through him, wreaking havoc on his mind. He felt like a nut-job chasing her around the city.

He arrived at her place in The West Village only twenty minutes later, a major feat considering the city's crowded end of day grid-lock. Thankfully, his driver knew the hidden short cuts. He took the front steps two at a time and buzzed her apartment number, 8B.

"Yes," he heard her say expectantly.

He waited a beat, then said gruffly, "Simran, it's me." There was silence on the other end. Then some crackle.

"What do you want?" she asked.

"What do I want!? We're not done yet! I need more time to explain myself."

More crackle, then static met his ear, then her voice, "Do you really?" she asked mildly.

"Um, *yes*. And did you really think we were finished?" he barked back. He was met with silence. He would wait, and he loosened his tie to get more comfortable, ready to loiter her doorstep until she came to her senses. *The gall of this woman,* he thought. Dropping pregnancy and cancer grenades left and right and then just disappearing. He finally heard the door click and relief flooded him as he swung into her building. He raced to the elevator taking it to the eighth floor.

When he got there, he immediately remembered that the floor only had two doors. One on one end where she lived and the other was to her business, *Lavish Your Events*. A large decal with the print, 'Best of The Knot, 2020,' was plastered to the door under the logo. He remembered Simran saying she was jumping through hoops to make that happen and he swelled with pride. She was so good at what she did, and he truly admired her for it. He was proud of her success.

❧❧❧❧

The knock came on her door, short and curt and she was prepared. Sabine had texted her a few minutes ago, warning her that he was on his way. She laughed and rolled her eyes at her sister's patronizing tone when she read it.

Taking a deep breath, she opened the door. She took her time sizing Foxy Lehigh up and down. Here was his all-business persona, and he was so, so fine. He was wearing a flawlessly tailored grey work suit that did nothing but accentuate his long, muscular legs and broad shoulders. His hair was tousled, pushed back from his forehead, and he was clean shaven. He'd loosened his deep lavender tie, one she recognized as a gift she'd given him before he left. She thought it would make the color of his eyes pop even more, and she'd been right as she noticed his piercing stare. Why was he so damn sexy ALL THE TIME? How did he do it? His face looked a bit haggard, though, and he wasn't happy at all. Obviously, they both hadn't slept well. She wished she could be smug about that, but all she wanted to do was go and comfort him. *Him!* The man who had hurt her.

She noticed his eyes travelling up her body and she became self-conscious. When she'd come home earlier, she'd thrown on a favored, cropped sweatshirt and matching joggers, the peach color faded from overwearing and washing. Her midriff peeped out and a shoulder was bare where the neckline hung wide. She folded her arms over her exposed stomach, not wanting him to see the extra skin there from her miscarriage, and she moved a hand up to smooth back some stray hairs coming down from her haphazard ponytail. When she glanced at his eyes though, she saw his pupils were dilated with that undeniable heat, and his face held an almost pained, wanting look—the evidence of his desire for her. She was both heartened and alarmed.

Down, boy, this is no time for that.

She cocked her head and said, "Hi," pleasantly enough. She had to keep calm. This was a second chance to cordially close the chapter on them and this time she would do it right. She was determined to, even though she still felt that undeniable connection to him. She'd talked herself back to being firm with herself when it came to Marc. What happened between them was too muddied, too much for her to mentally handle, especially when she had her dad to deal with.

He pulled his eyes from her to look past into the apartment. "You re-decorated," he commented as he saw the soft, barely-there pink walls in her foyer and vintage wall cornices painted in the same color. Then his eyes swung back to her. "You didn't tell me you were checking out of the hotel," he growled. "Can I come in?" She sighed, dropping her arm, letting him in. Oh, he was mad.

He took off his suit jacket, hanging it in the front hall closet. He slipped his shoes off, too, followed by his tie. She thought again how comfortable he seemed in her place, even though they had only been here together a handful of times. He looked around, rolling his sleeves along his strong forearms to his elbows. Simran caught herself staring and had to tear her gaze away from those arms, her own thoughts turning a little heated. If she wasn't careful she would completely undress him with her own eyes.

She gazed at her apartment, seeing what he was viewing for the first time. Simran needed a major change when they broke it off, so she restyled the whole look of her place. Taking the rich and elegant hues way down to a more relaxing vibe, the large living space was now painted in creamy white. The picture windows on the opposite wall bounced natural light off of it dramatically during the day. Sheer white curtains framed those windows and when open, created a dreamy cloud as the breeze blew, because the escapism was a necessity from her shitty reality and lonely thoughts. She'd even started carving a space out for the baby but was glad she hadn't worked on that too much, only just starting to think up nursery themes when shit hit the fan.

He glanced around appreciatively, noting some of her newer pieces of furniture, too, and walked to the windows to look out. He gently fingered the curtains, while the fall evening light played tricks with the airy material, creating an almost halo like effect around his head. Simran squeezed her eyes shut to the scene. He was *not* Prince Charming coming to rescue her.

"This is really nice, Simran. I love what you've done." She wanted to blossom with pride from his sincerity but didn't want to get carried away with her emotions.

"Thanks," she said curtly and shut the front door. But he continued with the compliments.

"I saw the sign on your door. You made the Knot's 2020 Vendor List. Congratulations, that's amazing and so well deserved." His eyes were so warm as he turned to her, his voice so sweet. There was awe in his handsome face, waiting for her to say something.

"Um, thanks. Yeah, you know, cross that off the list. Now onto next year's goals. They never end do they?" The enthusiasm in her tone sounded fake, even to her own ears. Her work goals were so far from her mind right now. She was still reeling from her dad's expectations of her and how real they were. How in the hell was she going to handle *that*? She'd been furiously looking for plane tickets to Mumbai before Marc arrived at her door.

"Simran, what if it's cancer?" he asked all of a sudden. Worry lines appeared on his forehead and he clenched his jaw tight.

"Then it's cancer," she said simply. "I'll find a really great Oncologist and go from there. I think I already know a few through the South Asian community." She shrugged her shoulders. She wasn't going to let him see how scared she was about it. Nor was she going to let him see how alone she felt.

"*Christ*, Simran, let me be here for you, whether that happens or not. I fucked up; I know. I got scared, but I now know what I want." She saw his lips tremble a little and his large hands open and entreating in front of him. She had to look away. *Oh lord, why?* Why did he have to make this harder than it already was?

"I got this. I'm taking some time off from work. I hired a new person for the time being and gave the nerds all the responsibility," she replied, trying to ignore his admission of messing up and wanting her back. "You should have seen them," she continued. "I think they went out celebrating after I told them I was taking a leave of absence." She was trying to joke her way through this one, but nothing was further from the truth. They were more than willing to take care of work, but the concern they had for everything happening in her life, from heart break to the miscarriage, and now the cancer scare, had them bereft of any funny business. All three had at separate times pulled her aside and told her they were there for her. They would keep business running as usual and would make her proud, she had nothing to worry about. If she needed anything they were just a phone call away. She didn't know what she'd done to have such an amazing group of people working for her. When she'd hired them a few years ago, she felt like the mother hen, coaching and teaching them the ropes, even making herself available for their personal life crises. But lately, they were the ones making her feel cared for. She realized she wasn't as alone as she thought she was initially; Sabine was here, too, and Tina would be by her side in a heartbeat. But the person she wanted the most by her was standing in front of her, offering it to her. She didn't want it this way, though, with the underlying pity.

He just shook his head and dropped his hands, walking over to the coffee table. "Simran, we need to talk this through—" He stopped when he glanced at her laptop screen. His breath hitched and he looked up quickly at her. "You're going to India?" he asked, his voice a little hoarse with shock as he saw the list of flights on display. *Crap.*

"Oh, yeah, just taking a trip to visit some family," she answered vaguely, coming to where he stood over her computer. She shut it with a snap and looked up at him. His face was still questioning, with his eyes darting back and forth between her own, trying to find the truth. She had never been good at keeping things from him and had never wanted to in the past. But now she had to. He didn't need to know about her family drama or her sense of duty and obligation to her father. He had some indication, but there was nothing he could do, even though he was all she still thought about, even after he broke it off, the baby loss—everything. God, the admittance of that was such a large, rough pill to swallow, and her heart felt like it was breaking all over again. But this situation with her father was all her and she had to figure out a way to make her life work with it.

20

Chapter 20

She wasn't telling him something. She'd already suckered punched him multiple times. What else was there?

"Yeah, I think it's just time for a change of scenery after everything. I need something different for me right now. I mean, you know what Lloyd Banks rapper extraordinaire said," she commented, leaving him to go into the kitchen.

"No, I actually don't," Marc said exasperated. Her loveable quirkiness was coming through but now was not the time for it.

"'If you stay in one place, you can only rap about one thing because that's all you know'," she quoted, as she came out with some sparkling water for them both. She handed him a glass, herself taking a huge drink, practically chugging it down, as her eyes peered widely at him over the rim. She was acting jumpy, and he wanted to get to the bottom of it.

"When do you get back?" he asked, and she shrugged, not giving him anything.

"What's going on, Simran? Why are you really going to India? For once, tell me the truth." And he immediately regretted his last words. Her eyes flashed and her gorgeous face puckered up with hurt. "I'm sorry, that was uncalled for," he said quickly. He saw her gulp, trying to keep her emotions in check.

"It's ok," she struggled to squeak out. "Like I said before, I should have told you about the pregnancy. You did have a right to know, Marc." It wasn't lost on him that she called him 'Marc' instead of "Marcus." Was he getting through to her? He shook his head, trying to focus on what she was saying to him. "I have to go to Mumbai. My dad is trying to get me hitched to my old boyfriend. Remember how I mentioned I was almost engaged? Well apparently, I'm on the road to my own week-long, loud, and crazy celebration to the guy I was almost engaged to six years ago." The bitterness was heavy in her voice.

"Wait, *what*!?" Marc felt like he couldn't breathe. Was this a joke?! If it was, it was cruel and ugly. But she was dead serious—her forehead creased between her shapely brows; her mouth set in a hard line. She was not happy about this either.

Marc felt his gut twist. This was so much worse than when he thought there may have been someone else. This was thousands of years of culture calling her back to the motherland to fulfill a duty she felt she had to uphold. He'd heard her in the past, listened to her when she briefly brought up marriage, her father, even the fact that arranged marriages still happened in her family. She was a confident woman, but he could tell she was unsure when it came to some parts of straddling both her Indian and American cultures. Never did he think it was easy for her, but he didn't think it would get to this point. Maybe he hadn't really known how dire the situation was. She acted so blasé most of the time, and truthfully, *he* never wanted to talk about marriage, so they never delved deeper. Was this his fault? All he could do in any of the instances where she felt uncertain, whether it was about her culture or something else, was try to be supportive, be there, and appreciate her for who she was. She was more than enough and anyone who couldn't see that needed a swift kick in the ass.

"Sims, talk to me," he pleaded. "Why is your father doing this to you? What about your sister?"

She sighed in frustration. "He's just trying to be a good Indian father. He thinks he needs to settle my future because I'm his responsibility as his daughter. It doesn't matter if I have my shit figured out—not that I do," she said that last part so quietly he almost didn't hear it. "But I think more than anything, as he's aging, he wants to make sure that both his family and business are settled into good hands. He's not going anywhere soon, the guy will probably live longer than any of us, but the idea makes him content. If I marry someone who has worked for him, someone who is familiar with our family and someone he can trust, then everything will be tied up in a perfect bow. He can retire, enjoy some grandkids, and do the whole *nana* (grandfather) shebang." She paused. "And Sabine, well, you've finally met her," she smiled softly. "The woman has always marched to the beat of her own drum and done so since we were kids. I think he might be a little afraid of her actually. Bottom line, he has no sway over her like he does on me." And her smile disappeared, her sullenness back, and he realized he didn't know as much as he thought he did.

Something was keeping her tied to her responsibility to her father.

"He knew about us," she continued. "The gossip mill started with all the Aunties last summer and finally reached him in India. Remember that barbeque in New Jersey?" She was referring to one of the last parties they had attended together at her family friend's home. "They all loved you, you know that. But he wasn't happy about it when he found out. He made it clear a few months back that he wasn't a fan of my personal life choices. I knew he was aware of us when he referred to me being mixed up with men who had certain reputations and wicked repercussions, you know, like the blackmail." She cringed as he sucked in air, his eyes going wide.

⌘⌘⌘

FOUR MONTHS AGO

Marc had been back in her life for a few weeks now. They were finding their routine and enjoying each other more than ever—both in the sack and out. What had she been thinking in not wanting to try things out with him? The warning call from Tina a few days ago was still fresh on her mind, and she'd done a bit of reconnaissance online (she hated herself for that), but Simran was starting to think she could let her guard down. He was so warm and attentive; had a sense of humor and intelligence ... essentially *all* the words in her vernacular that described an amazing man.

At that moment, she was lying naked in his bed, having just woken up to another bright, early summer morning. She stretched luxuriously, not having a care in the world, turning to look for him. He was always up before her and liked to watch her awaken. There was always a funny grin on his face every time she opened her eyes because he liked to see how long it took for her sleep fog to clear up. She usually had to twist around the bed for a bit, let her limbs move, stretch, then finally open her eyes to the day.

This morning, she opened them to an empty bed. She got out and found his button-down shirt from last night's charity event, haphazardly thrown on the floor with the rest of their clothes. She smiled as she picked it up, remembering how they couldn't get naked fast enough after ditching the party early. She put it on, buttoning up. Maybe he was going to surprise her with breakfast. She'd learned only a few days ago that he could make a mean omelet and sometimes liked to kick his chef out of the kitchen (to Chef Jon's alarmed look).

As she came up to the sitting area, she heard Marc's voice low and worried while he cradled his phone close to his ear. He was in pajama pants and a t-shirt. His broad back was to her and he didn't know she had crept up on him.

"No, no, it's ok. I'm here for you. I always will be, you know that," he said gently and with so much caring emotion in his voice. "I'm so, so sorry." There was a pause while he listened, running his hand through his hair. Then he said, "Yeah, I'm going to take care of it, you have nothing to worry about. I'll see you soon, ok? I'll make sure to plan a trip as soon as I can. I love you very much." He hung up and stood there, just looking at his phone, the tension bunching up his shoulders.

Um, come again?! Who was he talking to and who the hell did he love? She didn't think love was in the cards for them; although, what she was starting to feel for him was closer to that feeling than she truly wanted to acknowledge to herself. And he definitely behaved like he cared, too, even though they had never talked about it.

She cleared her throat, breaking the silence. "So, good morning," she said hesitantly, her heart beating uncontrollably in her chest, and her ears and cheeks burning from unsurety. He whirled around, his mouth open and his eyebrows almost up to his hairline.

"Sims!" he said in disbelief. He looked like she was invading his space and it was the first time she had ever felt unwanted by him. The feeling was deep and horrible, tearing at her.

"I can go," she blurted out, her instincts kicking in. She felt like she didn't belong there and turned to go back down to his room and grab her things. *What in the actual hell?!* Was Tina right? Was he fucking and ducking, now?! It sounded like he already had another woman on the side. Was he a cheater?! Well, this was new, important, and very screwed up information for her to have. She ran faster down the stairs, goaded by a 'fight or flight' response starting to consume her, and shit if it didn't feel all too familiar to the experience with Neel years ago. She practically leapt over the last few steps in her own hurry to duck out of this situation.

"Simran!" He chased after her and came to the room, shutting the door quietly behind him as he watched her scramble to pull on her bra. Her underwear was missing in action so she would just have to do without it. She kneeled on the floor in search of her sequined cocktail dress. Shit, where was it, and why hadn't she packed her overnight bag? Because they were in a hurry last night (her fault due to an impending work deadline) and she'd just let it go. *Stupid Simran, letting your guard down … couldn't even pack your own crap.* Would she have to go home in his clothes now? *Ugh!* Then she would have to smell him while she wore his clothes. Then she would feel like she had to launder his clothes. Then she would have to return his clothes to him. No wait, why did she have to be so polite about it? She would burn his clothes in a bonfire. *Perfect.*

"It's ok," she said quickly, her voice muffled in the fur comforter which had spilled onto the floor, keeping her mortified face from his view as she chased down her heels while only wearing a bra. "I should have known. You're a player. It is what it is. This has been awesome; *you* have been awesome. I was an idiot to think a perfect guy like you, handsome, smart, and used to having loads of different women, wouldn't have already gotten bored with me. Of course, there's someone else." She *knew* the last few weeks had been too good to be true. But why did he come to NY for her then? Talk about getting the major 'run around,' and she bit her cheeks to keep the tears from falling and lashing out at him. What an absolute dick. The anger she could deal with, but the hurt that surged so fiercely inside practically knocked the wind out of her. With some relief, she finally found her dress, wriggling into it while still on the floor. She just wanted to get the hell out of there. Let him wallow in his own bad behavior while she wallowed in a bottle of red and a pint of cookies n' cream.

There was silence. She didn't hear him move toward her, but felt his warm hands pull her by her arms to stand up. He brushed her hair from her face with such tenderness, she wanted to slap him, then kick him in the nuts. Why was he being so kind? It was cruel.

"Baby, *what* are you doing?" His face and voice were filled with gentleness, a smile trying not to break out on his lips. "There's no one else. I promise. We've talked about this. Well, actually, let me back-track, there sort of is ... that was my mom on the phone." Then seeing her tears, her lip starting to tremble, he said gently, "Please don't cry. I can explain." He waited for a reaction from her, his thumbs swiping at the tears that had managed to escape, then his hands slid up and down her stiffened form. When she finally nodded, having needed a moment to compose herself, he bent his knees to look into her face and asked softly, "And, you think I'm perfect?" This time he didn't hide his smile and it was so wide that it reached both his ears. He looked like a clown; the sexiest, most attractive clown she'd ever seen in her entire life.

Simran knew her whole face was beet red, and probably her neck and chest, too, embarrassed at thinking he was a two-timer. Clearly they weren't at a point where she trusted him one hundred percent and she felt awful. And now he knew she thought he was perfect, even without the complete trust. Trying to hide it was useless because the words were already out there, just flashing between them like a big, fat neon sign.

A little shakily, she said, "Marc, I'm sorry. I jumped to conclusions. Of course, that was your mother. But you could see how that would be misleading to me." She twisted some of her hair in her hand, feeling like an absolute loon. "And I think you misheard me. I said you're a "pervert," not "perfect," she fibbed weakly, looking down and biting her lip. "So, um, what's going on? Is everything ok with your mom? I mean, you don't have to tell me—"

His hoot of laughter came out deep and booming. She looked up to see him shaking his head at her. "Ah see, I have impeccable hearing and I know what I heard, baby. And I'm only perverted when it comes to you, sweet cheeks." He nuzzled her nose sweetly, while simultaneously rubbing her ass. "Your underwear is in my tux jacket pocket, remember?" he whispered, reminding her about what they had done the night before. It all suddenly came back to her. She'd teased him incessantly about his public persona—the one where his confidence and charisma captured everyone's attention; where he spoke with such authority and enthusiasm that he always collected a circle of admirers around him. It was such a contrast to what he was like when he was in a relaxed setting with her, or when it was just the two of them. He was an absolutely impatient beast, pulling both of their clothes off, sometimes not even taking the time to do that, then having his way with her. So, she wanted to see if she could make a crack in the "public Mr. Lehigh." After chugging enough champagne to make her daring, she'd gone to the restroom and removed her underwear. She'd returned to their dinner table and dropped them in his lap, giving him a naughty look. He'd been surprised, but then grabbed them with glee before anyone noticed the lacy, miniscule material, stuffing them into his pocket. Her intention had been to break him a little, but she quickly realized she was playing dangerously.

At dinner, he'd erotically felt her up under the immaculate white tablecloth with one hand, while casually enjoying his port and cheese plate, and calmly chatting up the head of a multinational corporation on the other side him of him. What had started out as a playful game had turned hot and heavy in a New York nanosecond, with Simran in a sexually frustrated haze. She had no idea what the elderly woman on her right, decked out in opulent furs and jewels, was even talking about. She'd been rambling on about being a child in India during the end of the British rule. All Simran could do was nod and agree with the older woman, because her brain had become mush with her body tingling and on fire. Hell, she'd probably agreed to the old biddy thinking India had been better off as a British colony. It was all she could do to not start gyrating in her chair in response to Marc's long, deft fingers, moving so articulately in and out of her. He was a master at this game, and their reason for leaving the event early—at her urging! And had she succeeded in making a crack in his public persona? His inability to keep his hands off her while they waited for his driver to pull up was victory enough. The sequins on her dress clicked hypnotically along her body to his feverishly roaming fingers, while his warm, heavy breathing against the back of her neck indicated him losing control.

A giggle burst out of her that she tried to stifle as she remembered her behavior last night. Marc continued, "And of course, you're changing the subject again. See, I know your tactics, Ms. Khan, you can't hide from me," he teased. Then he kissed her gently on the lips, whispering to her that her antics would always keep him on his toes, and she was pretty damn perfect to him, too; probably the best pervert he could ask for. Simran laughed and her body softened. She put her head on his chest while he stroked her back. She felt him murmur against her hair and she pulled back to ask him to repeat himself. "I said, I would never cheat on you. No matter what my past was, I've never been a cheater." Well, there it was, front and center. She could either take it or leave it. He was being totally honest with her; she could tell by the way he was looking at her so seriously now.

She breathed an "Oh," to him, putting her head on his chest again. She felt relieved and up until that moment, she hadn't even realized it had been weighing on her. All she knew was what he'd told her after that night in Brooklyn, which was that he had a womanizing past, had been with many, many different women, and that most of those flings ended on good terms. More importantly, he'd never wanted to get to know any of them more deeply until he'd met her. Other than that, he'd kept his explanation brief, and she was actually thankful for it. The sleazier stuff she heard from other's gossip (like Tina and her group of London friends, who meant well, but didn't know the truth). Shouldn't she believe what came out of his mouth if she was in a relationship with him? "I believe you," she whispered loud enough for him to hear and she felt him nod. And she did. She felt soothed now, but then horrified that she was making him comfort her when he clearly had pressing matters concerning his mother. She put her arms around his waist and started caressing his back, hoping to return the favor.

"Well … so, talk to me about your mom. Maybe I can help," she said to him.

He sighed, sitting on the bed, pulling her to sit next to him. He ran a hand through his hair anxiously, explaining a situation that unfolded a few years ago involving a former fling. He'd been too loose lipped with her at the time, something he learned not to do going forward so that his personal business wouldn't get into the press. He hated the gossip, but more than anything he didn't want anyone close to him getting hurt. He'd been careless at the time with a mindset completely under the influence of partying and he mentioned his mother to this woman. He told her she was single and lived in California by herself. A month later, his mom was seeing someone. She hadn't dated in a while, but this new guy just started in one of the pottery classes she taught at the community center and wormed his way into her feelings. When Marc had time to visit her and meet this new boyfriend, the guy had skipped town, managing to steal all her credit cards, jewelry, and ransacked her home office, looking for anything else of value. They got the police involved, but nothing came from it. The guy was elusive. Then his mom started getting weird letters in the mail, mentioning her rich party boy son and the secret photos they had on him. They wanted a handout, or they would leak everything to the press. They could only conclude it was the boyfriend and possibly someone else working with him.

Simran was shocked. "How much?" she asked, but it also dawned on her why he was so closed off or considered "cold" to the public.

"1.5 million," Marc said. Simran was floored. He had that kind of money lying around? Of course he did, he was loaded. It was something Simran really didn't put an emphasis on in their relationship. If anything, she tried to make him come down to her level at times, like standing in line for museum exhibits, instead of going straight to the front and mentioning his major donor status.

He continued, saying his private investigator tried to find the bastard, and that they were able to negotiate the amount down to three quarters of the original asking. He liquidated some stocks as quickly as he could and made the transfer. He got the photos back, thankfully, and hoped that was that. He looked at Simran hesitantly.

"You don't have to tell me," she said, grabbing his hand and squeezing, even though she was curious, without a doubt. She knew his reputation. She would definitely need to refrain from doing any more online searches of his past. That was something she had put a hard and fast rule on herself about because she didn't want to know (her recent and brief sleuthing being the absolute last time she dug around). It could only lead to trouble. But now, maybe she did want to know.

Marc's Adam's apple bobbed. "It's ok, I want to tell you. It was a multi-day party Bruce had thrown down on some private island off the Maldives. I don't know how drunk I was; I had done some recreational drugs, too. We were all high as kites, and," he swallowed hard again, "screwing like there was no tomorrow. I think I was with two women at one time. I just can't put the details together. One of them was the woman I already mentioned. At some point, the second woman, a friend of hers, had separated from the group and we couldn't locate her, not that any of us really noticed right away. But when someone did, she was unconscious at the bottom of a steep incline." He stopped there. "You have no idea, Sims, I flipped out. We all did. She just looked like a broken rag doll." He shuddered at the memory; his eyes glassy.

Simran nodded, squeezing his hand. "What happened to her?" she asked bravely. She didn't know what to expect, but good God this was worse than she could have imagined. Was there a death involved?

"She was so high and intoxicated that she just wandered off by herself, slipped and fell. That's the story and we stuck to it. No one was in their right mind to know what really happened. We called the Coast Guard and luckily they sent a chopper to fly her to a medical facility immediately. She survived, thank God, and didn't press charges or seek retribution. She was an up-and-coming Hollywood name at the time and didn't want the bad press. But the pictures I mentioned before were pretty incriminating. One was of us scrambling in horror when we found her and the other was of me with her, our hands all over each other a few hours before it all happened." He was silent for a bit, and she felt his stare on her face. "Should I continue?" he asked, haltingly.

Simran glanced up and saw a look on his face she'd never seen before. It was vulnerable, and so unsure. "Please, yes.

What happened?" she asked gently, pushing her hair behind her ears and giving him her full attention again.

"Well, long story short, my private investigator found out that the boyfriend was connected to my former fling. He's her step-dad." Marc shook his head at the idiocy of the entire thing. "They concocted this cockamamie scheme to get to my mom because they thought she had money, too. And she lived on her own, so she seemed like the perfect target. But they didn't find much, so they came after me. The photos were collateral, and they would try to ruin me if I didn't pay up. If my mom hadn't been involved, I wouldn't have given a shit. I don't care about my dirty laundry being aired out. But I couldn't do that to my mom. It's not her fault I made those poor decisions. Anyway, when I got the photos back, they were pretty grainy, like someone had been moving around while clicking away. They had to have been taken with a camera phone, so someone at the party had to have been the photographer. All evidence pointed to that woman, my former fling, and the step-daughter in this sick and twisted team." Marc stopped and sighed again. "We ended up finding her in Vegas trying to pull some scam on a few high-rollers. She was arrested and did some time in the state penitentiary. She also paid a hefty fine for black-mail. Now she's under constant observation by my investigator and she knows it, so I don't expect any more trouble from her. We still can't find her slimy step-dad, though." He got up and walked over to the window to look out. "The number it did on my mom—she was heart-broken, and then scared for her life and mine." He ran a hand through his hair then crossed his arms, still not looking at

Simran. "That was her just now on the phone. She got another strange letter in the mail, and it frightened her. She's worried this guy might be back to stir up more trouble. I've got to get my security detail working to follow her and keep her safe again. But she fucking hates not having her privacy. I'm a shitty son for putting her through this."

Simran saw the tension in his back again. She got up and went to him.

❧❧❧

Was Simran going to bolt now for real? He turned to her as she approached and tried to read her face. She'd seemed so certain that he was on the phone with another woman; that he was already in the middle of cheating on her. Based on his past, he really couldn't blame her for thinking that, but he hoped she could come to trust him. He would never do that to her and had never treated any woman like that before. And now this—this was a lot of information for her to take in. Maybe she would reconsider wanting to be with someone with this kind of sordid history, way worse than what she already knew about him. But he couldn't keep this kind of thing from her. He felt like an open book, exposed, a feeling he'd had with her since they first met. She had a way of making him want to tell her things without worrying about what she would do with the information. But what would she do now?

"I'm glad you trusted me enough to tell me." Her voice was filled with tenderness as she cupped his face with her slender, cool hands. "I'm sure you aren't a shitty son. It doesn't seem like it from what I can tell," she smiled kindly. "I'm sorry you and your mom are going through this again. I wish I could help." Sincerity made her voice so quiet and her dark eyes black and shiny. He pulled her to him, hugging tight, smelling her scent so familiar to him now. She had no idea that just being able to tell her was in fact helping him. It felt freeing to be open with her. Bruce knew, so did Jon, and, of course, his mom, but knowing that Simran knew, and she didn't find him disgusting, made him feel lighter. She accepted him for who he was.

Marc stared at Simran across her living room in disbelief. "So, how exactly does your dad know about that, Sims?" he asked cautiously, trying not to jump to any conclusions. Had she told him? No *fucking way*. She wouldn't have done that.

"Give me a break, Marc." She rolled her eyes. "My dad has his own ways. He's well connected internationally because of his company," she said pointedly and she was right about that. He must know a lot of the right people to get his hands on that kind of information because Marc and his Publicity team did their damnedest to keep that situation under wraps. Inevitably, some of it leaked, though, and his mom's life had been impacted. People in her community relentlessly asked her personal questions, and her class attendance was over-crowded; everyone wanted a piece of her salacious gossip. It'd been a rough year for Gail Lehigh in her tight knit community, and Marc felt completely responsible. But, Simran's dad must have also been fishing for it. He was trying to make Marc look like the bad guy to her.

"Anyway," she continued, "my dad has been talking to Anil seriously again."

"Anil?" Marc asked, trying to rack his brain for any recollection of this person.

"Yeah, I've never mentioned him before by name, but Anil Patel is the guy from that one serious relationship of mine from back in the day. He's someone I've known almost my whole adult life. He's a few years older than me and still works for my dad's company. We met when I was finishing up at NYU and visiting Mumbai on a break. At first he was like an older brother to me, but it turned into this weird, romantic attraction because he reminded me so much of my father and I felt that if I could be with this person, I would forever please my dad and my family." She rolled her eyes again. "I was young and didn't know who I was. It's a South Asian guilt thing and—"

"Wait, what? Explain that please," he said abruptly, shaking his head. He really wanted to know where all of this was coming from and she was actually opening up about it.

She huffed, her face twisting into irritation. "You really want to know?" He nodded, his arms crossed over his chest now, and she pursed her lips in concentration. "Mm, how do I describe this?" she asked herself, one arm folded over her belly, the other twisting the hair of her ponytail as she thought and stared out the window. Then she continued, "Ok, so, it's this obligation to fulfill a duty for the best of one's family, which goes hand in hand with the need to obey and listen to your elders. It's pretty common amongst South Asian offspring and it doesn't matter if you're living in India, America, or freaking Antarctica. I felt it then and I think Anil felt the same way. He wanted it to work too because he was tight with my dad and pretty much like the son he never had. It was almost too perfect. We dated long-distance for almost three years." She looked away, then said awkwardly, "I mean, I did end up caring for him and he was my first real lover. But he cheated on me while he was working in Germany, that's why things ended. But, I thank the universe every day that things ended up the way they did because I would *not* have made a good, Indian wife, only working part-time, managing a household and kids. That's what he expected of me then." This was the most he'd ever heard her talk about her past relationship. She'd always shied away from it, acted like it wasn't a big deal. And now he understood why cheating was such a hot button topic for her, why her spikes came out whenever she saw him interact with women from his past or felt like she couldn't trust him 100 percent. He closed his eyes and shook his head again. He almost felt like he didn't know her at all. His thoughts were a chaotic mess with all of this new information: 'South Asian guilt', cheating, Anil Patel. Then those thoughts came crashing down and he had a new feeling of dread as his mind worked around that name.

"Anil Patel, Head of Consumer Relations at your dad's company?" he asked. There were a million Patel's in India, but how many were there with that exact same name and who worked in her dad's organization; an organization that he and Bruce had worked with first-hand? He still hoped her answer was no.

"Yeah, he's been in that role for a few years now." she said surprised.

He sighed a little defeated. "I know the guy. I'm pretty sure it's the same person. He worked with us a few years back to smooth out some infrastructure issues when we opened our club in Mumbai." Anil Patel was smart, successful, had his head on straight, and reluctantly, Marc could think of nothing bad to say about him from that time. He recalled that Anil had shown them around, giving them an authentic taste of Mumbai. He'd really seemed like a great guy, if not a little conceited, mentioning multiple times that he was well on his way to the top of the company.

Marc knew without a doubt that Anil wasn't the right guy for Simran. She was smart, caring and fiercely loyal. But she was also strong-willed, and at times fucking exasperating. The truth was, all combined made her a complicated and beautiful person inside and out with so much to offer the world around her. It sounded like Anil would crush that beauty and all that made Simran who she was. She'd be forced to live a life that wouldn't allow her to continue to blossom and explore herself. And only a self-centered dick would do that.

The blood thundered into Marc's ears so forcefully that he felt a little dizzy. He could feel the jealously rising from the depths of his chest and spreading to the tips of his appendages. The stiffness made him want to punch a wall. "So, now what?" he tried to ask calmly. "It's been years since you were with Anil and it sounds like he wasn't the guy for you then. Is this *South Asian guilt* still something you consider so important to you that you would consider that dick again?" he asked, feeling a little nauseous and disgusted. *Fuck.* Why had they never touched on this before?

"Well, you're one to talk," she said scornfully, crossing her arms in front of her chest. She was right, he'd acted like a dumb prick with her, too. "Not that it's any of your business, but I *am* going to see him. I need to see this through. I honestly don't know what will happen. I'm over him and have been for a long time. My dad thinks it's a good idea and only thing I'm capable of doing long-term—being a good Indian wife and all that goes with it." She visibly shook as she spoke. "My dad has no confidence that I can continue with my business. He's proud of me sure, but thinks I'm just dabbling and having fun. I'll eventually realize I need to settle down soon. I mean, I *am* old, can't you just see me withering away in front of you?" she asked, her eyes wide with mock horror, her sudden, throaty laugh music to his ears.

ೋೋೋೋ

She saw emotions chasing each other across his face: humor, frustration, hurt. *Oh God, I'm hurting him.*

"Just so we're clear, Simran, you will *always* be my business," Marc said firmly, his eyes stormy. Simran's heart did a summersault in her chest and she told it to calm the fuck down. He'd forfeited his right to any of her business when he dropped her months ago. "So, you *are* seriously considering Anil?" he asked condescendingly. Self-importance oozed from him with his wide-legged stance, and his arms were still crossed over his chest. An eyebrow raised questioningly at her and she wanted to wipe that asshole look of his face, but simultaneously run into his arms.

"Well, no. I don't know. No," she waffled back and forth. What *did* she want? If someone had asked her a month ago what she was doing with her life, she would have rattled off a short list that included running her business and raising a child. But now, things were utterly screwed and she wasn't so sure about what she wanted anymore. She'd briefly considered the marriage to Anil as an escape from her painful reality in NYC, but also knew that wouldn't be fair to either of them. Maybe if she saw him again in person, the answer would drop into her lap. She sighed, frustrated tears welling into her eyes. "I just need some time to figure this out and I need to go because it's the right thing to do. I'll know when I get there." She knew this wasn't the same Simran that Marc knew from their past. This was so-unsure-of-everything-in-her-life-right-now Simran, completely unhinged after all of the crap she was wading through.

He came to her, crossing the barrier, to take her cool hands in his overheated ones. Just that touch made her feel lighter, even though she'd dropped another bomb on him. Her chin fell to her chest in relief but she didn't want him to see it.

"Simran," he asked gently, "Can your father really do this?" He lifted her chin to look at him. His eyes were so charged with emotion she thought she would get lost in those deep pools of cool blue.

"I think he's already got the ball rolling," she answered, not moving away from him. In fact, she leaned into him, the familiar security his broad chest offered was a beacon to her. He didn't even hesitate. He pulled her to him, crushing her body to his, rubbing his hands up and down her back, trying to sooth and comfort her. And Simran thought it felt right that he was here.

She in turn crumpled into him, resting her head on his chest against the strong beat of his heart. It was as if all the hurt and mess of their situation didn't even come close to what her father was trying to do. She wanted nothing more than to close her eyes and stay in Marc's strong arms forever.

"Marc, I—" she started to say, but he shushed her. He cupped her face with both hands, his look so tender, and he leaned down to kiss her, stopping her words. He was gentle, brushing his lips over hers, softly licking, then sucking, while whispering for her to shush again. Then he became more fervent, with his warm mouth opening over hers and it was like he was trying to claim her as his. She returned the kiss, falling under his spell like she always did. But was it a spell? No, this was real, this connection of theirs. She already knew that and there was no denying it despite everything, just like that first time when he came looking for her in NYC. Simran's hands automatically moved to his neck, and up through his hair, feeling the smooth locks under her fingers.

His mouth continued to move over hers, coaxing her to fully open her own, while his hands slid to her waist, keeping her up against him. He whispered to her how beautiful her lips were, how much he missed kissing them. The hum of his words vibrated sweetly on her, and she had to break away before they lost complete control. She tried once, twice, but his mouth followed hers possessively. She finally put her hands to his hard chest, and shoved him back, freeing herself. She panted as his lips found her neck instead, sucking hard on his favorite spot like he was branding her, reminding her that she was his. His hands pushed greedily up her sweatshirt to stroke her bare back while he crushed their hips together and she felt his hard length pressing into her belly. She inhaled sharply, her body becoming warm jelly, and she started panting with need. Now she was losing control and she didn't care.

He pushed her back up against the wall, pinning her wrists in one hand over her head as he grinded himself into her. His other hand pulled the hair band from her hair and her curls tumbled down in a wavy mess around her shoulders. He combed through her strands, murmuring he loved her new hair, and wanted to see her in nothing but her curls. She arched to him, moaning, emotions flowing through her. Tears escaped her eyes; a response to missing him these last few months, and probably forever in the future.

"Did he ever make you feel like this, Simran?" Marc groaned softly into her ear, his lips nipping her lobe, then moving down to gently bite her neck, kissing her bare shoulder, then coming back to her neck as he breathed heavily and continued to press his hard body into hers. He was talking about Anil, and never had it been this way. Never had intimacy been so out-of-this-stratosphere-satisfying with anyone but Marc, where her blood just sang into a crescendo until it detonated like explosions inside her. She shook her head, unable to form an intelligible word. His hand slid to her front under her shirt, skimming her belly and navel and stopped to rest below her breasts, his thumb grazing back and forth on the undersides of her soft flesh. She arched even further to him, her body on auto-pilot, wanting him to squeeze her breasts and pinch her nipples. He did just that as she gave full, guttural moans of pleasure which mingled with his own appreciative sighs.

He moved his hard length into her sensitive mound and her hips pressed into him reflexively. "Are you wet, baby? I bet he never made you this wet," he rasped into her neck, knowing that she was completely sopping in her underwear now, because that's what he did to her. "Do you feel what you do to me, kitten?" His voice was hoarse, his breathing heavy, while he moved his hard cock erotically up and down her groin. Then he answered himself back with a hiss while she moved her hips into him again, and her animalistic moan of utter lust didn't even sound like herself in her cozy living room. His hand started to glide down her belly, trying to seek entrance into her pants, and she wanted it. She wanted his fingers in her wetness, wanted him to assuage the need she had tried to ignore for the last few months. But, as soon as she felt his prying fingers brush her bandages, her desire careened to a halt.

"Marc, *don't.* You *have* to stop!" she sobbed. Her eyes were open now as she realized that they could not do this. She didn't think her heart was ready and her body wasn't even close to fully recovered.

Her panicked tone had him stop short. His eyes flew wide as he looked at her, his heavy breathing rapid and shallow as he tried to control himself. And in his eyes she saw possessiveness then regret. He dropped her hands and stepped back to give them space. The air swooshed over her body and she felt empty and cold.

"*Christ*," he said under his breath. "I'm so sorry," he said louder, a hand shaking as it raked through his hair. "Simran, I—lost control there," he tried to explain, his voice still rough, his face anguished. Now all Simran could think was *I want you to lose control, and I want to go down with you.* Then she wouldn't have to think about anything but their incredible fucking. "I have so many feelings in me. I've never felt this way about someone else." He took another shaky breath while his hands balled up at his sides, as if he was trying to refrain from grabbing her again. "Sims, I care for you so much. Fuck, baby. I don't know what being in love feels like, but I'm betting this feeling, how my heart feels like it'll stop beating knowing you might not be with me, that's what I imagine this is."

Simran's own heart stopped for a few beats, then coasted high, completely undone by his unexpected words. The apples of her cheeks burned hot, and she looked down, unable to meet his eyes. She couldn't say the words back to him. Everything was so raw at that moment after seeing him, feeling him, that she needed to protect herself from the hurt he'd inflicted months ago which was starting to return in full force.

It'd been so long since she'd experienced emotional difficulty to the point where she couldn't react openly. In fact, how she was feeling now was similar to how she reacted in the hardest situation she had ever had to endure in her life: her mom's death so many years ago. Back then, she had withdrawn into herself, just leaving a Simran-shaped shell for others to interact with. She had needed Tina's help to bring her back to herself.

Right now, standing in front of Marc, she wasn't broken like that of a child who just lost a loving parent. But her head was certainly a jumbled, sad mess and she wasn't ready to reveal herself to him; she stubbornly didn't want to, either. He didn't deserve to know what she was thinking, even though she knew she harbored the same feelings of love for him, felt them deep in her soul. She just wasn't so sure it was the right decision for her. She needed time to process what would surely be the casting aside of an important part of herself if she accepted Marc back into her life, ignoring her father. And did she even have it in her to forgive him? Did she even want to?

She peeked up to see him watching her intently, his brow furrowed, his jaw clenched and ticking, waiting for something, anything, from her.

All she had in her at the moment, to let him know that she heard his declaration, was give him a nod and whisper, "Ok."

She knew without a doubt, though, that no matter what happened, it wasn't over between them. It wouldn't be until there were no feelings left. She would bawl like a baby all over again when and if that happened because she didn't think she would ever be over Marcus Lehigh.

ধন্যবাদ

Thank you so much for taking the time to read Simran and Marcus' story. I hope they've become as loveable to you as they are to me. If you enjoyed the first half of their journey together, please leave me a review on Amazon or Goodreads! And guess what? You'll have the chance to continue rooting for them in **Love's Liberation**, book 2 of my Liberation series; out Summer 2022 just in time for your next beach read!

About me:

I love romance, travel, and exploring the South Asian identity. As a South Asian American woman, I write about what I know, having been brought up in the US and living from coast to coast. When I'm not taking my readers on a journey of love and self-discovery, you can find me enjoying my family, friends, crafting, dancing, and I'd be lying if I didn't add Netflix binge-watching!

Follow me on social media to find out what I'm reading, and what I find fascinating in the world of the South Asian American/Western/Female diaspora. Or drop me a line ☺, I'd love to hear from you!

www.instagram.com/ktsromance/
www.facebook.com/KhushiT.S
Dhanyabad—Thank you—and XO,

Khushi T. Saha